Murder of Inspector Hine

by

David Dowson

# CHAPTER 1

The county's shadows swallowed a cop whole, his death unleashing a deadly wave of chaos.

# CHAPTER 1

## Murder at the Train Station

THE LAST MURDER in Sumter County was on Christmas eve of 1999. A blonde lumberman was drugged, shot, and hauled into his garbage with a bullet in his brain. Having busted and prosecuted the murderer, less murder cases graced the books of the Sumter County Police Department until that breezy night.

Detective Inspector Shepherd got the phone call while stuck behind the steering wheels of his rickety iridescent blue Volkswagen Jetta. He was about a mile away from his apartment in downtown *Glover Ridge*. The call was from the head security guard at the *Olive Boulevard* train station. A man is killed and hung upside down on the gantry of the station's overhead bridge. It is something the Police must see before the media ever gets a chance.

In the company of Detective Sergeant Brown, Detective Inspector Shepherd hit the scene at exactly 8:15 pm. He's humid and tense at the same time. A murder at the train station means a great deal of danger to a typical Sumter County cop. It could leave a question mark on their competence. It could fetch them serious trouble.

Detective Shepherd's forehead contorted into a grimace when the details became clear. The surprised cop found it hard to force the glaring reality down his turgid throat, but he did. What was unfolding before him wasn't just a murder. It was the murder of a cop. A good cop. Again, Detective Brown further studied the corpse to be sure it was who they thought he was. He was the one; Detective Inspector Ray Hine, who was with them in the same briefing room four hours ago.

In a case as sensitive as the murder of a cop, what Detective Inspector Shepherd feared most was the contamination of the crime scene. With a strong will to retain the crime scene and keep every potential evidence intact, he swiftly ordered the establishment of perimeters, with the bustling camera-armed journalists kept at a distance. Shepherd wondered what could be more alert than the American press—they almost hit the scene before the cops. He couldn't take chances.

Things swiveled around the train station in a blink of an eye. Ghosts of tension and urgency lingered in the air —reeking of a blend of curiosity and unease. The initially free platforms suddenly became a labyrinth of caution tape as red crime scene markers mopped the ground, wading off commuters.

Before the paramedics hit the scene, Detective Inspector Shepherd had gained ample time to pore over the corpse, enough to make a handful of extracts. Ethically, he needed the green light of the forensic identification unit to conclude the identity of the murder victim, but he subconsciously created no room for shabby procedures that'd add nothing but theoretical weight to the investigation. He's the best Homicide detective in Sumter County Police Department and knows when exactly to lean on the shoulders of the forensic team. The corpse before him was Detective Hine. He had worked with him for 12 years—he'd never mistake him for someone else. If he could miss any other detail, his badge was enough to give in his identity.

Getting enough clues from a mere feel of Detective Hine's temperature, it was obvious that the cop must have still been breathing in about two hours or less from the discovery of the body. The scene and post-crime handling of the body by the murderer exhibited all shades of a well-executed murder. It wasn't a careless hit-and-run attack. It never looked like one. Detective Hine's throat was slit from ear to ear and his body was tied in a figure of four using water and strain resistant Polypropylene ropes that kept him firm and stiff—cold as a snowball and heavy as lead. Even in death, his face spelt courage and bravery—he never stopped looking like the fearless and brazen cop he was.

"You said you found this at 7:50?" Detective Inspector Shepherd asked the security guard towered by his side. His name tag read *Sheldon K.* He was the same guard who phoned the cop. The head security guard of *Olive Boulevard* train station.

"Yes, 7:50," Sheldon responded, his eyes not leaving the corpse.

"As the head security guard, were you notified of the presence of a corpse around the station's premises?" Detective Shepherd asked, studying Sheldon's face.

"I discovered the corpse while on my routine check," he responded in a subtle tone that spelt confidence. "Routine check?" Detective Sergeant Brown chipped in, his baritone suddenly caked with utmost curiosity.

"We do that immediately after the last train of the day hits the gears."

With a notepad and a ballpoint pen in his hand, Detective Shepherd turned to Sheldon again. "When did the last train leave?"

"7:45."

"Carriage!"

"240 passengers."

"Destination."

"South Nottingham."

"How long will it take that train to hit South Nottingham?" Detective Shepherd asked.

"9:30," someone behind Sheldon responded. He was his colleague. Chubby and blonde. Unlike Sheldon, he was on mufti.

The arrival of the paramedics in the company of the forensic team interrupted Sheldon's interrogation. But Detective Shepherd made the necessary orders. He ordered Detective Brown to dispatch an emergency surveillance team to the train station at South Nottingham. Intercepting the train suddenly became utterly necessary.

"Secure that train station before the driver hits the break. No one enters…no one leaves."

"Roger that," Detective Brown hollered, amid a weak salute.

Sheldon and his colleague still lingered around, perhaps hoping to be further interrogated by Detective Shepherd. Upon noticing their presence, the anxious cop patted Sheldon firmly on the shoulder.

"Get me onboard, Sheldon. Right at the security room. I want to see the CCTV footage of this station for the last 48 hours."

Detective Shepherd had high hopes. Hopes of getting clues, enough to get his team tangible leads. But, only the forensic team could tell if the hope would hold water or not. With his 20 years of experience as a homicide detective, Detective Shepherd saw the clean games the murderer played—the signs were glaring. However, it was only the forensic team that could tell how flawlessly the murderer rolled his dice.

Images of the living Detective Inspector Hine flushed through Detective Shepherd's head. Hine's clean-shaven face and the brown eyes behind his rimless specs flooded his mind's eyes. No one could say what he did to deserve death but whatever it was can be dug up. That stood firm as Shepherd's biggest hope—even as he caught himself reminiscing on the birth of their friendship. To him, that's what they were; two cops who shared more than mere colleagues would.

"I rather chase justice than greenbacks," Detective Hine mumbled, taking a long sip from his tumbler. He was at the pub down the hill. Yeah. Everyone who's been in Sumter County for more than four months would know about the pub at the base of the hill where Detective Hine's was often found.

"Then every county cop should own a castle built with justice," the cop in a mufti and cowboy hat responded to Detective Hine, sagging his head backward in laughter. He was mocking the nearly drunk Detective Hine.

"Then you'd never stand a chance at the honors, Klaus," Detective Hine further challenged, tossing his vodka-filled tumbler to the air as if for Klaus to admire.

Sergeant Klaus rifled a stare in Detective Shepherd's direction, his face squeezed into a grimace and his lips curved in anger. "Of what monetary use are they?"

"Glory, Klaus…"

"You let go of your family, risk your life and combat crime in exchange for fanciful medals and call that glory? Come on, cop. Wake up. You think that matters more than a better paycheck?"

"That's better than a bag of cash that'd never bring honor to your name," Detective Hine roared back, maintaining his stance despite the backlash and occasional laughter from other eavesdropping cops.

Detective Shepherd sat back, watching the two cops trade words. That wasn't the first time he caught Detective Hine advocating unparalleled service to the Police Department. All round the clock, the loyal cop stressed the need for county cops to pursue honor and glory over money. Possibly, that was the reason he was the third out of the only three cops in the Sumter County Police Department with a Service Medal. All he tried proving to Inspector Klaus Benson, a Swiss criminologist-intern-cum-cop, was the essence of being an honorable cop over a one with a fat purse but no glory. Despite his alcohol addiction, Detective Hine's commitment to the service had won the hearts of many. He was the Chief's favorite. A cop of cops.

A brief conversation with him after the argument at the pub marked the beginning of his bond with Detective Shepherd and the thought of that bond gave the cop every reason to track down Hine's murderer. It was enough reason to pull everything together to foster justice for Hine's death. He was the least of Sumter County cops to die in such a terrible manner. "Anything we can hold onto?" Detective Shepherd asked the hand-gloved man on black leather jacket the moment he snuck out of the van. He's Gary Murdoch, the head of the forensics team. Tall, slender, blonde and slightly bearded.

"Apparently, yes. But at this point I'm afraid I'd have to avoid being conclusive as much as possible," he announced in his typical Mexican-accented English.

"What are the clauses?" Detective Shepherd queried, wincing clumsily.

Gary chuckled. "I think we both know what's at stake, Detective," he said and turned to the spot where Detective Hine laid before being hurled into the ambulance on a sleek trolley. "These prints are quite shabby," Gary announced, looking away.

"I can't agree more," Detective Shepherd admitted, adjusting his waistband as his eyes rifled for the crowd of murmuring journalists. "I believe you can spot the clues better than I do…I mean, that's why we're a team."

Gary adjusted his specs and led Detective Shepherd further away from where they stood. Perhaps, he yearned to clear the air and make things plain without squeezing fear into the minds of other eavesdropping cops.

"I'm afraid this might be a tough one, Detective. All we've gathered so far are yet to hit our labs but we all can see the glaring decoys," he said and looked over his shoulder. "Whoever did this is no novice. It was well-played."

"But why Hine?" Detective Shepherd asked. He couldn't say if his question was a rhetoric or directed to Gary but he just watched his mouth spill the question.

"We can get all the answers we want if we don't take chances," Gary assured, taking off his latex gloves. "Ballistic analysis is a great way to begin and we'd get to dig up everything worth digging up. Just play your part!" "Are we really doing that bullet bullshit again, Gary?""We have to…"

"That damn thing hardly pulls through for me…Bolivian shells, Mexican cartridges and all that junk. The last one led to a 45. Blowback owned by a Russian vegetarian in Sochi…" Gary pocketed the gloves he just pulled off his hands and docked his arm on Detective Hine's shoulder. "That's why we coexist, Detective. Again, play your part!" "Consider the "what ifs", Gary! This could fetch some horrible news. I'm afraid the council, if not the mayor herself, would come around."

"This is why I've made zero promises, Detective," he fought back, his tone slightly higher than it had ever been. But he was sure he wasn't shouting. "I can't ignore the setbacks littered all over the crime scene. We've got a murder scene quite decorative but with almost nothing to hold onto. It seems our murderer was quite the Houdini of crime. He's left behind an illusion of emptiness, with little or no substantial evidence to work with." "But it makes me wonder how possible that shit can be!" Gary chuckled again. This time, it was a fake one. "Nothing's impossible for these people. Every day, cops grow wiser in their approach to criminal investigation and so do criminals when executing crimes. We've detected a high possibility of the use of nitrile gloves and plastic suits that'd leave no fingerprint or DNA trace behind. I could be right that the few we've detected could be Hine's but that's subject to confirmation."

Detective Shepherd held his head in his palms, his ears perked up as Gary's words hit him hard. "Do you ever see this getting fixed?"

Gary leaned closer. "The 1947 Black Dahlia Murder was solved and so was the JonBenèt Ramsey of the '96. I believe we'd get something to bite on, Detective."

*We'd get something to bite on!*

This thought suffused Detective Shepherd's head until Gary wambled out of sight. All he wanted was to have Gary confirm his convictions and the forensic expert did just that. Shepherd saw the rareness in the handling of the corpse and suspected signs of a well-planned and almost untraceable crime. But like Gary said, he had no reason to trash all his hopes. All he'd need to have even a lone clue is a single mistake from the murderer's end.

Detective Shepherd was on the phone with the Chief of Sumter County Police Department when Detective Brown signaled for his attention.

"You might want to see this, Inspector." The dark-skinned man was lost in the midst of cops, swiftly glancing back and forth as if on the lookout for someone. He seemed to be on alert as his reddened and deep-set eyeballs bulged out of their sockets.

Detective Brown introduced him as an eyewitness who claimed to have seen Detective Hine and some tall white-skinned man heading out of the train and strolling towards the bridge whose gantry his corpse was later found hanging. However, Detective Brown had just one reason he felt the man's narration on the case shouldn't be taken seriously. He was a homeless.

Detective Shepherd waltzed closer, his eyes pelting the man's frame in a fine-tooth comb. The man's frail face was etched with lines of seamless struggles. His bulging eyes held a sense of vibrancy, perhaps one birthed by his victory over the cruelty of the unforgiving street life.

As the aroma of deprivation reeking from him wafted through Detective Shepherd's nostrils, he couldn't help but stare through his threadbare backpack. The cop didn't miss a detail from the homeless man—from his weathered jawlines, tattered white-turned-gray blanket, worn and spineless books to his screen-less denigrated silver pocket wristwatch. It'd take an ocean of carefulness for the anxious cop to believe whatever the man would say.

"Are you sure you know who we're talking about?" Detective Shepherd asked, gawking at his frayed face.

The man nodded to Detective Brown, "From his description, I do, " the man replied with a weak chuckle that exposed his uneven set of brown teeth with inescapable dental tartar.

Patiently, Detective Shepherd watched him ruffled through his backpack as if looking for something. Detective Brown shuffled backward, maintaining a distance and assuming a defensive stance at the same time. "Isn't it the hero cop you're talking about?" he asked, splaying a faded newspaper. The old-looking once gray newspaper had turned yellow and although it had blurred and smudged letters, the pictures on it were still recognizable. Drawing Detective Shepherd's attention to the picture, the man tapped one of the faces in the picture, "that's him. Right?" Detective Shepherd maintained his gaze on the paper for a few more seconds before nodding in admittance. He recognized the picture and only needed to find Detective Hine's name stuck within a few paragraphs to be sure he was right.

The newspaper was published in the summer of 2011. He could recall the event vividly. It was the day Detective Hine received his first Service Medal from the then Mayor. It was an achievement that came a week after he saved seven kids from a burning bungalow in the outskirts of Glove Ridge. He was truly the hero of Sumter County. But, questions creased through Detective Shepherd's head. They came in tens. But at the top was the question; *why is he still keeping the newspaper after a decade?* "You saw him in this station tonight?" Detective Shepherd asked.

The man nodded swiftly. "I did see him walk through the door of the train with a takeaway cup of coffee."

"Alone?" The man thought for a while and shrugged. "With lots of other passengers.""The train moved with him in it?" "No!" the man disagreed. "He moved out." Detective Shepherd traded quizzical glances with Detective Brown and turned to the man again, his chest tightening up.

"You claimed to have seen him around the bridge with a white-skinned man," Detective Brown interjected.

He nodded.

"Please, you'll have to answer me audibly. Did you see Detective Inspector Hine with a man around the bridge tonight?" Detective Shepherd paraphrased. The man kept mute, studied their faces suspiciously and then headed back to staring blankly at nothing in particular. "I saw Officer Ray walk towards the bridge," the man finally responded. He turned to the direction of the bridge and concluded. "In the company of Jackson."

"Who's Jackson?" Detective Shepherd hushed, leaning closer.

"He's the mechanic at the edge of the boulevard."

## CHAPTER 2

### The Order

A TRAIN TRIP TO SOUTH NOTTINGHAM after 7:00 pm was too late. But since it had to do with Aunt Lindsay, Detective Inspector Ray Hine couldn't hold back. He murmured an *I'll be back in a moment* to the potbellied Sergeant at the exit door of the Sumter County Police Department's briefing room and rifled for the gate. In a jiffy, the sound of his rickety scooter droned the car-less road as he rolled down the hill.

At the Olive Boulevard train station, he squeezed himself through the entrance of the lounge and made for the crowded counter ahead. As the receptionist settled off the old lady on the line, his piercing eyes were on the massive information board by his left. The last trip to South Nottingham was less than 20 minutes away from takeoff. He wasn't too late.

"Get me on the last train to South Nottingham," Detective Hine said to the smartly dressed lady over the counter.

Like the blushy waitresses at the luxury restaurant in Central Bornwood, she gave him a wide grin that came with a blend of surprise before responding. "That might be a long ride, Sir!"

Detective Hine shrugged it off with a stern face.

"Are you sure you'd like to go that far tonight?" she asked again. Perhaps, she couldn't read the gesture on the cop's face.

He plonked his badge on the counter in a fairly loud stud. "Detective Inspector Ray Hine. Sumter Police Department. Special assignment," he announced, trying not to sound intimidating in any way.

"Oh. I-I-uhm." she stammered.

"Come on. It's cool."

"But would you like to…"

"A minute more might be too late, Miss Courtney" he said as soon as he palmed off a dollar bill. He finally caught a glimpse of her name tag.

"There you go," Courtney placed a ticket before him. "Safe trip!"

•

If Detective Hine is found without a bottle of rum, he'd never be found without a takeaway cup of coffee. Wherever the former is prohibited, he settles for the latter. To him, having something to lift his spirit wouldn't be bad. Besides, the trip to South Nottingham was a long one.

After getting a cup of coffee from the coffee dispenser, Detective Hine staggered through the sea of commuters as the deafening honk from the train droned the platform. The hurrying cop kept both a close and cautious watch as the rat-race unraveled. The cackle of children. The subtle chime of ticket machines and turnstiles. The tick-tocking of hard heels against the worn tiles. The reeky smell of sweat and the acrid odor of diesel and cleaners. The overall feel of the typical Olive Boulevard train station hit him hard.

A few meters to the door of the train, he tightened the grip on his brown satchel and hastened his step as the departure announcement came aloud. He had long been expecting it…at least to be sure he wasn't on the wrong platform.

"Attention, please, the train departing from platform 5 is Vanwood 456 enroute to South Nottingham. All passengers are requested to board the train and…"

"Excuse me, Sir" a voice cracked into Detective Hine's ears, followed by slow but insistent taps on his arm. A small but firm sensation.

"How may I help you, boy?" he quizzed as soon as he veered around.

It's a boy. He looked like one who'd easily fall within the thirteen to fourteen years age bracket. As light beams from the train mopped his frame, Detective Hine had a clear view of him—from the topmost strand of his red-haired head to the top of his funky black boots. He was blonde and charming; with a body that looked twice his age. He wore a white Mickey Mouse tee atop a jean jacket folded to his ankle and black boots coated with layers of dirt. His narrow eyes were nearly swallowed by his puffy cheeks and reeked of terror as he struggled to explain himself to the curious cop.

His face held streaks of sweat and a mere stare at his heaving outward-bulky inward-tiny chest would show that he must have been running—he was breathing through his teeth.

"Is everything okay?" Detective Hine asked, his glimmering eyes ransacking the direction the boy euchred out from.


"I-I…" the boy stuttered, his jittery eyes looking across his shoulder like he was being chased. He began a slow but steady jerky-trembling.


Outside the train, Detective Hine's gaze met no sign of danger. Not a pint. Everyone moving towards the train held no sign of suspicion nor danger. Not even his eagle-eyed visual raid could spot a clue. Swiftly, he leaned downward, so low that his head and the boy's remained on the same level. An eye contact was rudimentary for him to have a peek into the boy's fear.


"Hey, look at me," he requested, swiveling the boy's face in the direction he kept staring at. "What's your name?"


"Come on. He's gonna harm her. We gotta go now! Please," he further pleaded, completely ignoring the cop's question.

"Listen to me, boy," he placed his hands firmly on the boy's shoulder. "You've got to calm down and tell me how exactly I can be of help to you…what's your name?"

The boy shrugged and pulled a stern grimace. "My mom. You've got to save her…she's in danger. "

"What's wrong with your mom? Where is…"

"Come on. We've got no time…" the boy insisted, grabbing Detective Hine by the leg. The act had already won the attention of the passengers in the particular couch. It made the cop feel awful.

Meanwhile, Detective Hine's fate approached a crossroads when the announcement came aloud.

"…we're three minutes from departure. Secure a seat and get ready for your trip…"

"My mom needs your help, please. She's with some bad dude out there in the dark…"

Detective Hine peeked through his wristwatch and headed back to the boy. "Where are they?"

"The bridge. The lights are out!"

Detective Hine turned backward only to find a bunch of eyes marauding his frame. He pulled the halfway closed door aside and stepped out, following the boy's lead.

"Come on. Please, you've got to save her…" he hollered.

"But I…"

"Come on. Save her. Isn't that what cops do?"

The mention of *cop* took Detective Hine aback. He held no sign of being a cop around him. Briskly, he scanned the boy's face and looked ahead, right into the direction the boy was about leading him toward.

"How did you know I'm a cop?"

The boy responded with a nod towards Detective Hine's midsection. He had flung his black jacket to one side in a way that exposed his badge.

"You have to save her. Isn't that what cops do?"

*Yeah. That's what cops do!*

"Alright," he hushed and took to his feet. "Take the lead…" he mumbled to the boy, nodding ahead. The two didn't go more than three steps when the train's door closed and it began moving. Hine just missed the train.

It was quite confusing for the cop. Aunt Lindsay is his only distant relative and was reportedly stuck in the hospital bed just after she got her first stroke attack. Getting to see her at South Nottingham that night would have meant a lot to both Hine and his dying aunt but he just couldn't watch the boy's pleas water away.

The first plan was to pair him with a security guard who'd check up on his mother but none was at sight. In all indications, it seemed like he equally trusted none of the guards but him. Detective Hine kept ahead as the train increased its speed, leaving him behind.

"Come on, hurry up," he murmured to the boy who was a few steps behind him. His pulse skedaddled as he breathed helplessly. He was charged up. The inflow of air must have been so hard on his tiny lungs. The bridge was at the next bend, quite closer but perhaps for the boy, it was more.

*You can do this!*

Detective Hine prayed.

\*\*\*

Detective Hine saw everything but not the man silhouetted at the edge of the bridge. All his alerted eyes and perked up ears went for the low feminine groans and grunts oozing out of the dark. His stainless steel Glock was trained forward in his signature Navy Seal position, ready to take down whatever took a wrong move.

But, he didn't see the move when it came right after him. First, he heard a loud stud. What he heard next was a breezy run. The third sound the cop heard was a gunshot. Not a brassy and insistent one that'd hover in the air seconds after being fired but one from a silenced gun. He's heard, seen and used a few of these guns himself. Noiseless but as swift as the speed of light. The slender bullet swam right into Detective Hine's upper arm, keeling him off balance. His Glock fell to the ground in a clatter.

His only succor left him.

"Dishing out justice to the unworthy can be quite easy, Inspector Ray," a coarse baritone announced as Detective Ray sprawled on the floor, fighting to hoist his frame.

His eyes grew blurry and his pulse leapt. An aura of terror swept his frame as he struggled to see through the dark. Few minutes ago, it was only drizzling but on every move he made, his entire perimeter got slapped by mammoth balls of rain. A thunder-less but heavy rain. One that'd decide his fate.

Again, he let out a manly groan. The second bullet tore through his knee. It crept through his tough jean pants and danced through his knee cap, sending a sharp pain to the edge of his spine. The footsteps got more audible but kept fluctuating. The figure made circles around him, watching him whimper as the excruciating pain ran deep in his frigid veins.

"All my life…the law made me destitute," the figure said and paused for a moment. "In my very home."

The voice was deep and thunderous but held flickers of sorrow and pain. Every word harbored an emotion and even while submerged in a trance of pain, Detective Hine could feel them.

"W-hat do you want, you asshole?" Detective Hine blotted in anguish. All he wished was to tower his limp and kick the fearless figure in the balls. His bravery boiled but his legs were watered. He had the will but no power to wield it.

The figure volleyed a hard kick that sent him back to the ground, crashing like a pack of cards, all his efforts to gather more strength.

"What I wanted was survival, Inspector…I couldn't have asked for more…but. It. Was. Dead. On. Arrival."

In a flash of white, Nathan's face blanketed Detective Hine's mind's eyes. Yeah. Nathan. The boy on the train. That was his name. Even in pain, Hine still recollected it. The cop will recall that getting to the bridge was only an effort to save his mother from trouble. To save her life. To do what's expected of every cop. But, there was no sign of him nor his mother. They vanished like clouds shattered by the harshness of the scorching sun. They left him in a bout he never bargained for.

The figure's voice kept fluctuating. Now, it'd sound like a murmur right into Detective Ray's auricle and some seconds later, it'd come off like the honk from a speed train 5 miles from the bridge. However, the utterly weak cop caught some more lines from his pain-coated words before his eyelids slammed against each other.

"I want to be free to take the fight to whoever drew the line without sparing a single bigot."

He heard that clearly. The figure squatted right beside him. He could feel the warmth of his breath. The rain was long gone. It left not even drizzles behind. Perhaps, it was done watching off Hine's chances of ever living again. But the pain unraveling within his core stuck…it crept all over his frame like a thick skin…like a rush of epinephrine. A flow that'd never wear away.

"I want to end the existence of a sect of people who enslave other sects with cuffs and laws just for sinning differently." He ended the statement with yet another shot. This time, to Hine's left knee. To leave him completely limbless.

Detective Hine watched himself wear away as each second faded. His mind got blown by a tsunami of endless thoughts—but more like they were about dissolving into a perfect symphony. His head grew hazy but his memories came clear. His limbs went powerless but his heart exploded with whispers from the floor of his soul. Something more powerful was knocking.

Dreams. Memories. Struggles. Victories. They all fell in place as his eyes grew dimmer. The lump that crept on the walls of his throat dissolved into his tracts and the rush of epinephrine nosedived. He heard dozens of kicks to the side of his head. The last thing he felt was the coldness of metal from the base of his neck—it came with sharp piercing pain that got him kicking. It was the same pain that tugged the last lump of energy off his frame.

The last stroke.

"The hunter is hunted!" the man laughed.

# CHAPTER 3

## A Thin Dot

*"AT THE EDGE OF THE boulevard."*

T hat was where the homeless man said Jackson lives. He further gave a physical description of the said Jackson but couldn't say what he does nor the exact apartment he lives in. On that note, Detective Shepherd's first assignment came clear.

*Find Jackson.*

Olive Boulevard is the least of the league of metropolitan areas in Sumter County. Instead of condominium complexes or high-rise towers, the fairly busy but tranquil boulevard is home to dozens of single-family homes and townhouses. It expands to the end of Barney Avenue and unfolds as far as 512th Street. It is home to dozens of people working at the train station and looking forward to cutting transportation costs.

However, the boulevard is home to the Sumter County Library, an iconic structure that sparks up traffic on the roads of Sumter County in summers. The library is known for being the home of President John Kennedy's high school archive—it holds the biggest and most sacred collection of the former president's books as a high school kid with a dream of pursuing Law in the Harvard of the 1940s.

Detective Shepherd made it to the buildings a few blocks away from the library. Two out of the three were empty. It had to be its own adjacent, then. Detective Shepherd had a faint intuition that they'd bump on something tangible across the arrays of buildings by the left.

Detective Inspector Shepherd and Detective Brown stood outside the unassuming apartment, their hearts pounding with anticipation.

The house is sleek but solid and as American as pie. It's a perfect combo of brick and siding, creating a pleasing blend of traditional and modern aesthetics.

The front yard showcased a lush green lawn that extended to the electric pole at the edge of the walkways. A pathway of interlocking pavers led from the sidewalk to the front porch.

While its oversized windows are framed in clean white, the roof is pure aluminum with asphalt shingles. Clearly, it complemented the neighboring houses in a way that harmonized the architectural beauty of the entire neighborhood.

With a swift nod, Shepherd and Brown stormed into the house, their eyes scanning every corner for any sign of Jackson. They meticulously searched each room, peering into closets, lifting cushions, and examining every surface for any clue that could shed light on the elusive figure's identity. But their efforts yielded no trace of a man named Jackson. Instead, they discovered that the house belonged to a Mr. Phil, a perplexing revelation that left them questioning the accuracy of the homeless man's account.

Perplexed, Shepherd and Brown turned their attention to Mr. Phil, who had returned home during their search. Chubby. Six-foot-three. Brown-haired.

Detective Shepherd approached him, his eyes piercing with determination, ready to extract any information that could help them solve the case. He bombarded the confused looking Phil with questions, probing for any connection he might have had with Detective Hine.

Yet, to their frustration, Mr. Phil vehemently denied any involvement or knowledge of the murdered officer. More shocking is his claim of not being aware of the murder of a cop at the train station.

"Not even heard of it on the news nor in the newspapers!"

Phil shook his bulky head, "No. Too busy for tv time. Too unstable to grab a newspaper…never actually liked the print media."

As the detectives concluded their questioning, their frustration mingled with disappointment.

The promising lead had turned into a dead end, leaving them back at square one. Reluctantly, they left Mr. Phil's house, their heads filled with unanswered questions and a lingering sense of defeat. Detective Shepherd felt messed up and used by someone he felt he shouldn't have even listened to.

Just as Shepherd and Brown were about to step into their car, Detective Shepherd's phone rang, shattering the heavy silence. He glanced at the caller ID—Gary Murdoch, the head of forensics. With a glimmer of hope, Shepherd answered the call, stepping away from Brown to hear the crucial information.

His heart raced as Gary Murdoch's voice filled his ear.

"You might like what I've got for you, detective," Gary chortled.

Meanwhile, the same Gary had earlier explained that the forensic examination had yielded unexpected results.

All the DNA and fingerprints found at the crime scene belonged to Detective Hine himself, a perplexing revelation that only deepened the mystery.

However, the post-mortem examination was yet to be concluded. In Gary's words, it held the potential to provide a breakthrough.

Shepherd's mind whirled with conflicting emotions—relief at the progress made, yet frustration at the lingering questions. The tantalizing possibility of catching the killer was overshadowed by the enigma of Detective Hine's inexplicable presence at the crime scene.

He knew that the laboratory held the key to unraveling the web of deception, and he vowed to meander with Gary Murdoch to delve deeper into the forensic findings.

**\*\*\***

Laboratories are eyesores. The stench it reeks can roast intestines. But, at this point, Detective Shepherd didn't mind.

As he stepped into the sterile laboratory, the scent of chemicals and the soft hum of machinery enveloped him. Gary fetched him at the door and they lounged into a lengthy conversation, dissecting every detail of the examination results. Shepherd's eyes darted between the lab equipment and the determined expression on Gary's face, their discussion growing more intense with each passing moment.

Gary's voice, tinged with a mix of excitement and gravity, filled the air. He confirmed that the DNA and fingerprints found at the crime scene undoubtedly belonged to Detective Hine, raising unsettling questions about his involvement. But the most significant revelation emerged from the post-mortem examination—the murderer shared Detective Hine's left-handedness and possessed the same black hair.

"Anatomical analysis makes it clearer than crystals. The positions of the cuts are enough to give clues," Gary said.

Shepherd's mind spun with possibilities, trying to reconcile the facts with the mysteries that still shrouded the case. The pieces were slowly fitting together, but the image they formed only deepened the darkness of the enigma.

Detective Shepherd clenched his fists, frustration seeping into his bones. How could Detective Hine's own DNA and fingerprints be present at the crime scene? Was it a cruel twist of fate or a deliberate attempt to mislead them? The questions gnawed at him, taunting his relentless pursuit of the truth."

"Gary," Shepherd's voice trembled with a mix of urgency and despair, "we need answers. Deeper and clearer answers. How is it possible that Hine's body prints are the only evidence m at the scene? What a sick game with us."

Gary's eyes met Shepherd's, mirroring the turmoil etched on the detective's face. "I wish I had all the answers, Shepherd," he replied, his voice laden with empathy. "But we have to consider the possibility of manipulation. Someone wants us to understand that Detective Hine's murderer isn't just untraceable but flawless—murdering a cop without leaving behind a trail of evidence behind is a daunting feat."

Shepherd's mind whirled, contemplating the implications of such manipulation. Was Detective Hine set up, or was there a deeper, more intricate plot at play? He felt the weight of the investigation bearing down on him, a heavy burden that threatened to consume him whole.

"What about left-handedness and the black hair?" Shepherd's voice carried a mix of desperation and determination. "Are these clues any more reliable? Can they lead us to the true identity of the killer?"

Gary's gaze hardened, his voice resonating with conviction. "We've analyzed the hair samples extensively, Shepherd. The killer is undeniably left-handed, just like Detective Hine. And the black hair found in Hine's nostrils matches his own. It's a distinct characteristic we can't ignore."

Shepherd's mind raced, connecting the dots and forging new paths of inquiry. He couldn't shake off the nagging feeling that there was something more significant hidden within these clues, something that would unlock the truth and expose the puppet master pulling the strings.

"This murderer, Gary," Shepherd's voice grew quieter, carrying a mix of determination and grief, "they knew Hine. They knew him intimately. Left-handedness and black hair are personal traits. We're dealing with someone who shares a deep connection with our fallen comrade."

Gary nodded solemnly, the weight of the revelation settling heavily upon him. "You're right, Shepherd. Whoever did this didn't just take a life, he probably violated the bonds of trust.

The determination in Shepherd's eyes flickered, reigniting with a fierce resolve. He would dive deeper into Detective Hine's life, his relationships, and the secrets he may have carried. Every thread, no matter how faint, would be pulled, unraveling the web of deceit that threatened to consume them all.

As Shepherd prepared to leave the laboratory, the room seemed to vibrate with unresolved tension. The answers they sought were tantalizingly close, hovering just beyond their grasp. But Shepherd knew that the truth could be a double-edged sword, capable of shattering illusions and exposing painful realities.

With the weight of his mission pressing against his chest, Shepherd turned to Gary one last time. "We'll find the answers, Gary. We owe it to Detective Hine, to ourselves, and to every officer who wears the badge with honor. The dark forces at play may think they can hide in the shadows, but we will bring them into the piercing light of justice."

Gary's gaze met Shepherd's, a silent pledge passing between them. They would not falter in their pursuit of the truth. With determination etched on their faces and a fire burning in their hearts, Detective Shepherd and Gary Murdoch shared a steadfast resolve.

As Shepherd stepped out of the laboratory, a sense of urgency coursed through his veins. He knew that time was of the essence, and every passing moment brought the killer closer to slipping through their fingers. With each step, he replayed the evidence in his mind, searching for any hidden connections that could guide him towards the elusive culprit.

\*\*\*

Back at the briefing room, where it all began, Shepherd called upon his team, assembling them in the briefing room. Detective Brown had long slumped into the armchair beside Detective Shepherd.

Their eyes were filled with a mix of curiosity, anticipation, and the unspoken pain of losing one of their own. Shepherd took a deep breath, ready to unveil the discoveries that had been made.

"There's danger lurking around," Shepherd's voice rang out with unwavering authority. "We're dealing with a clever and calculating murderer. The evidence at the crime scene has taken us on a twisted path, leading us back to Detective Hine himself. But we will not be deterred. The killer shares his left-handedness and black hair, suggesting a deeply personal connection."

A ripple of murmurs spread through the room, a collective realization of the gravity of their task. Shepherd continued, his gaze sweeping across his team, making sure each member felt the weight of the responsibility.

"We will leave no stone unturned. We will delve into Detective Hine's life, his cases, and his relationships. Every lead, no matter how insignificant it may seem, could be the key to unraveling this web of deception. Together, we will bring the truth to light and ensure that justice is served."

Shepherd's words hung in the air, their significance sinking into the hearts of his team. They were united in their mission, bound by a common purpose. Each investigator would contribute their expertise and relentless determination, pooling their resources to expose the malevolent puppet master orchestrating this intricate dance of death.

As the team dispersed, heading off to their assigned tasks, Shepherd retreated to his office. The weight of the investigation bore down on him, threatening to consume him in its insidious embrace. But he would not falter. The memory of Detective Hine's dedication, his unwavering commitment to justice, fueled Shepherd's resolve.

In the solitude of his office, Shepherd allowed himself a moment of reflection. He thought of Detective Hine, a man respected and admired by all, whose life was snuffed out too soon. He remembered the sound of Hine's laughter, the warmth of his friendship, and the unwritten code that bound them as brothers in arms.

"Rest in peace, Ray," Shepherd whispered, his voice tinged with a mixture of grief and determination. "I promise you, we will bring the one responsible for this heinous act to justice. Your sacrifice will not be in vain."

The room fell silent, as if the walls themselves mourned the loss of a great detective. But in that moment of profound stillness, a spark of determination flickered within Shepherd's heart. He knew that the path ahead would be treacherous, filled with obstacles and unforeseen dangers. Yet, he was prepared to risk everything to uncover the truth, to expose the dark heart that lurked in the shadows.

With the first chapter of their investigation coming to an end, Detective Inspector Shepherd gripped the edge of his desk, his knuckles turning white with resolve. The stage was set, the players were in position, and the game of cat and mouse was about to begin in earnest. The grave suspense hung in the air, promising twists and turns that would push Shepherd and his team to the limits of their abilities.

\*\*\*

Shepherd stared at the board in his office, covered with photographs, timelines, and red strings connecting the pieces of the puzzle. The faceless killer seemed to taunt him, his presence lurking in the shadows of each photograph. Determination burned within Shepherd's chest as he vowed to unmask the puppet master and expose their malevolent game.

Days turned into sleepless nights, and the pursuit of leads took Shepherd and his team through the darkest corners of the city. They delved into Detective Hine's past, meticulously examining his cases, searching for any connections that could lead them closer to the truth. They interviewed friends, colleagues, and even those with criminal records who had crossed paths with the fallen detective. Each encounter unearthed fragments of information, adding to the growing mosaic of the investigation.

In the midst of the relentless pursuit, Shepherd found solace in moments of introspection. He couldn't help but wonder about the motive behind the murder. Why would someone target a respected and competent detective like Ray Hine? What secrets did he carry that had led to his untimely demise?

As the days turned into weeks, Shepherd's frustration simmered beneath the surface. The lack of tangible clues gnawed at him, leaving a bitter taste in his mouth. But he refused to succumb to despair. He knew that a single breakthrough, no matter how small, could tip the scales in their favor.

One rainy evening, Shepherd found himself standing alone on the desolate streets, raindrops mingling with the sweat on his brow. The county seemed to reflect his turmoil, shrouded in an aura of mystery and uncertainty. It was in these moments, amidst the chaos of the investigation, that his mind wandered to the victims—the lives forever altered by the killer's actions. He couldn't shake off the weight of responsibility, the unspoken promise to bring closure to grieving families.

The ringing of his phone pierced the night, jolting Shepherd from his contemplation. He answered the call, his voice edged with a mix of anticipation and weariness. It was Gary Murdoch on the line, his voice laced with urgency.

"Shepherd, we've made a breakthrough," Gary's words cut through the air like a bolt of lightning. "We've discovered something that could turn the tide in our favor. Meet me at the lab immediately."

Shepherd's heart quickened its pace as he hurriedly made his way to the laboratory. The rain intensified, pounding against the windshield of his car, as if nature itself conspired to heighten the tension. With each passing mile, Shepherd's mind raced, conjuring possibilities, and bracing himself for the revelation that awaited him.

Upon arriving at the lab, Shepherd found Gary hunched over a microscope, his eyes shining with a mixture of excitement and trepidation. The room buzzed with a symphony of scientific instruments, creating an atmosphere of urgency and anticipation.

"What have you found, Gary?" Shepherd's voice trembled with a mixture of hope and anxiety.

Gary turned to face him, a small vial clutched tightly in his hand. "Shepherd, we analyzed the fibers found at the crime scene—the ones we initially thought were inconsequential. They don't match anything we expected."

Shepherd leaned in closer, his gaze fixed on the vial. "What do you mean, Gary? Are you saying there's another piece to this puzzle?"

Gary nodded, his voice filled with a newfound determination. "The fibers belong to a rare and distinctive fabric, Shepherd. It's not something commonly found in everyday clothing. I cross-referenced it with our database, and there's a match—a match that leads us to a secret society known as the Obsidian Order."

Shepherd's eyes widened, his heart pounding with a mix of intrigue and apprehension. The Obsidian Order was a shadowy organization rumored to operate within the depths of society, dealing in clandestine activities and wielding immense power. They operated in secrecy, their actions hidden from prying eyes, making them a formidable and elusive adversary.

"What is their connection to Detective Hine's murder, Gary?" Shepherd's voice quivered, his mind racing to piece together the intricate web of clues.

Gary's voice dropped to a hushed tone, his eyes reflecting a mixture of concern and determination.

"Shepherd, we've discovered evidence that suggests Detective Hine was conducting an undercover investigation into the Obsidian Order. He had infiltrated their ranks, gathering crucial information that threatened to expose their activities."

Shepherd's breath caught in his throat, the revelation sending shivers down his spine. Detective Hine, a trusted officer, had been entangled in a dangerous game, unbeknownst to his colleagues and even his closest friends. The stakes of the investigation had just skyrocketed, plunging them into the heart of darkness.

"We have to tread carefully, Shepherd," Gary cautioned, his voice filled with the weight of responsibility. "The Obsidian Order is a force to be reckoned with. They operate in the shadows, manipulating events to suit their own agenda. We need to determine who within the Order had the motive and the means to eliminate Detective Hine."

Shepherd's mind raced, his thoughts colliding like crashing waves. The pieces of the puzzle were slowly falling into place, revealing a sinister truth that threatened to engulf them all. The murderer's actions were not merely driven by personal vengeance but tied to a larger, more insidious plot—one that involved the Obsidian Order and their dark machinations.

The gravity of their task settled heavily upon Shepherd's shoulders, but he refused to be crushed under its weight. Determination flared within him, igniting a fierce resolve to expose the truth, bring down the Order, and avenge the fallen detective who had paid the ultimate price.

"We won't rest until we unravel the secrets of the Obsidian Order," Shepherd declared, his voice filled with steely resolve. "We'll dig deeper, follow every lead, and expose their sinister activities. The killer may have believed they could hide within the shadows, but they underestimated our tenacity. We will unmask them, no matter the cost."

As Shepherd and Gary locked eyes, a silent understanding passed between them. The game had reached a critical juncture, and they were prepared to risk everything to unravel the web of deceit. They knew that the path ahead would be treacherous, fraught with danger and betrayal, but they were bound together by a shared purpose—to bring justice to the fallen and expose the truth hidden in the depths of darkness.

But within that darkness, a glimmer of hope flickered—a beacon of light that promised to guide them through the storm.

With the promise of grave suspense lingering in the air, Shepherd and his team must embark on a perilous journey into the heart of the Obsidian Order, their determination unwavering, their resolve unyielding.

But, when the loud honk of a lumber truck shattered the silence in the neighborhood, Detective Shepherd knew he was lost in sleep. He was dreaming. He had long dozed off right at his untidy workstation.

"What is the Obsidian Order?"

# CHAPTER 4

## Morris Lodge

T EMPLAR SOLACE LEANED against the cold brick wall, his eyes fixed on the towering figure of Walter Tyndale. The fairly lit room was suffused with an air of secrecy and trepidation. The scent of aged leather and ancient parchment filled the air, mingling with the faint aroma of freshly brewed coffee wafting from a nearby pot. Solace's fingers twitched involuntarily, his nerves on edge, as he clutched the envelope containing his initiation instructions.

It was time.

Walter Tyndale, a man of commanding presence, stood before him, exuding an aura of authority and mystery. Dressed in a perfectly tailored suit, his silver hair glinted under the dim light, matching the steely glint in his eyes. A thin smile played upon his lips, hinting at the secrets he held close. He's huge in heart but minions in size. He's barely five-foot-three and has a dark scar that stretches from the back of his neck to the base of ear, crawling a bit into his cheek but not too prominent if not deeply stared at.

"Templar Solace," Walter began, his voice low and gravelly, "you have proven your loyalty and commitment to our cause. Today, you shall take the final step into our esteemed ranks."

Solace's heart pounded in his chest, a mix of anticipation and dread. He had known little about the organization when he first met Walter at the McDonald's franchise in Sumter County. Back then, he had been a private investigator, seeking a job as a security guard. But Walter had seen something more in him, something dark and malleable, and had offered him an opportunity that was both terrifying and enticing.

A chance to groom the villain in him.

The memory of his first murder assignment flashed through Solace's mind, a chilling reminder of the path he had chosen. He had stalked the casino owner, his heart thudding in his ears, the scent of fear mingling with the pungent odor of sweat. The man was innocent and gentle, not worthy of being snapped by death but orders needed to be obeyed.

When the moment came, Solace had struck, his gloved hands wrapping around the man's throat, squeezing the life out of him. The sight of the lifeless body, swathed in cellophane, had left an indelible mark upon his soul.

Now, as he stood before Walter, the weight of his actions pressed upon him. Deep down, in the recesses of his mind, a flicker of conscience sparked, urging him to warn the unsuspecting initiates about the peril they were about to face. But to reveal such secrets would be to sign his own death warrant.

It's a death sentence.

Loyalty was the watchword within Walter's circle, and betrayal was met with swift and merciless retribution. It's a bottomless dungeon. No way out.

As Solace's thoughts swirled, Walter extended a hand, offering him a small, ornate key. The touch of the cold metal sent a shiver down Solace's spine. He took the key, the weight of it heavy in his palm, a symbol of his newfound allegiance.

"Wear this key with pride," Walter intoned, his voice a low rumble. "It opens the doors to the path you have chosen, a path only a chosen few may tread. The secrets you will bear are not for the faint of heart."

Solace's gaze flickered to the ornate doors at the far end of the room. They were made of dark mahogany, adorned with intricate carvings and symbols that seemed to writhe in the dim light. Behind those doors lay the initiation chamber, the final test of his loyalty.

A stage he couldn't boldly tell if he was prepared for.

The sound of footsteps echoed through the hallway, growing louder with each passing second. Solace's heart raced, and he turned his attention back to Walter.

"Remember, Templar," Walter whispered, his voice a mere breath, "we do not take betrayal lightly. Your actions today will shape your destiny."

Before Solace could respond, the doors swung open, revealing a group of wide-eyed initiates, their faces a mix of excitement and apprehension. Solace pulled a nearly invisible smirk. Deep within his core, he didn't just pity them but wondered what promises Walter made to them. Just like he did to him.

The scent of incense wafted from the chamber, mingling with the nervous perspiration of the initiates. Solace's eyes scanned the group, his gaze lingering on their hopeful expressions, their anticipation of what lay beyond those imposing doors. His heart ached with the weight of the knowledge he carried, the danger they were all about to walk into.

As the initiates filed past, Solace caught sight of a young woman, her eyes brimming with innocence. Her slender fingers trembled as they brushed against the folds of her cloak, her lips moving silently in prayer. A surge of protectiveness washed over Solace, intertwining with the guilt that gnawed at his conscience.

Walter stepped forward, his voice resonating with authority. "Welcome, initiates," he greeted them, his eyes glinting with a mixture of pride and secrecy. "Today, you will embark on a journey that few are privileged to undertake. The path is treacherous, but the rewards are immeasurable. It's like the sky. No beginning. No end. "

The initiates exchanged glances, their excitement tempered by a hint of apprehension. Solace knew that behind those doors awaited not only the knowledge of ancient rituals and hidden truths but also the darkness that had consumed him.

One by one, the initiates passed through the doors, disappearing into the hallowed chamber. Solace watched as they vanished from sight, swallowed by the abyss of uncertainty. The scent of incense grew stronger, its heady aroma mingling with the electric tension in the air.

Solace's hand tightened around the key, his knuckles turning white. A torrent of conflicting emotions surged within him. Should he warn them? Should he break the cycle of violence and secrecy? The cost of such an act would be immeasurable, not just for him but for the innocents who dared to tread the path he once chose.

As the last initiate disappeared into the initiation chamber, Solace felt a presence at his side. He turned to find Walter's piercing gaze fixed upon him, an unspoken understanding passing between them.

"You feel it, don't you?" Walter's voice was low, his words laced with an eerie calmness. "The burden of knowledge, the temptation to save them from the abyss."

Solace swallowed hard, his throat dry. "Walter, there must be another way," he said, not believing that those words came out of his mouth. "We don't have to sacrifice more lives. There's too much blood on our hands already."

A shadow flickered across Walter's face, his gaze darkening. "You were warned, Templar, weren't you?" he said, his tone carrying a mixture of disappointment and resolve. "Loyalty demands sacrifices. We cannot turn back now."

Solace's mind raced, his thoughts a whirlwind of despair and determination. The overpowering scent of incense filled his nostrils, mingling with the metallic tang of regret. He knew the stakes, the price of betrayal, yet the flicker of hope in those young eyes haunted him.

Before Solace could utter another word, a deep, resonating gong reverberated through the hallway. The sound seemed to pierce through his resolve, each beat echoing with finality. It was the call to the initiation, the final act that would seal their fates.

Walter's gaze bore into Solace, his voice carrying a chilling warning. "Remember, Templar, the path you walk has no escape. Once you cross that threshold, there is no turning back. Choose wisely."

The weight of Walter's words settled upon Solace's shoulders, his hands trembling as he grappled with the decision before him. A gust of wind swept through the corridor, stirring the air and brushing against his skin like a phantom touch.

Solace took a deep breath, inhaling the scent of incense, feeling its tendrils wrap around his senses. The touch of the cool wind against his skin grounded him, reminding him of the world beyond the confines of this clandestine organization.

A surge of determination coursed through Solace's veins, mingling with the fear that had taken residence in his heart. He knew the risks, the danger that awaited him should he choose to defy Walter and the path he had reluctantly taken. But he also knew that to remain silent would be a betrayal of his own conscience, a sacrifice of his humanity.

Gathering his resolve, Solace met Walter's gaze with steely determination. "I won't be a pawn in your game any longer," he declared, his voice firm. "There's blood on my hands, and I won't let more innocent lives be lost."

Walter's expression hardened, the mask of authority slipping momentarily to reveal a flicker of concern. "You know the consequences, Templar. There is no escape from the organization."

A hint of a defiant smile tugged at Solace's lips. "Maybe not, but there's still a chance for redemption. For justice."

As the initiation chamber beckoned, a battle of wills raged within Solace. The scent of incense hung heavy in the air, mingling with the metallic tang of uncertainty. The weight of his decision pressed upon him, threatening to suffocate his resolve.

With a final, determined nod, Solace turned away from Walter, his footsteps echoing through the corridor as he strode toward the exit. The shadows danced on the walls, whispering secrets that had been concealed for far too long.

Walter's voice, filled with a mix of disappointment and warning, followed him. "You'll never truly escape us, Templar. We will find you."

Solace paused at the threshold, his hand gripping the handle of the heavy door. He glanced back, meeting Walter's gaze one last time. "Perhaps," he replied, his voice laced with determination. "But I will spend every waking moment fighting against the darkness you've embraced."

With those words, Solace stepped into the outside world, leaving behind the twisted path he had walked for so long. The taste of freedom tinged the air, mixing with the scent of possibility. The warmth of the sun bathed his face, a reminder that there was still light beyond the shadows.

But as Solace walked away, a lingering sense of foreboding remained. He knew the organization would come for him, their pursuit relentless. He had crossed a line, defied the unspoken rules, and betrayed the code of loyalty. The danger was far from over, and the battle for redemption had just begun.

And so, Templar Solace, former member of the dangerous organization of Freemasons, stepped into a new chapter of his life, haunted by the scent of incense, the touch of secrets he could never fully escape. The shadows of his past loomed large, intertwining with the hope of a brighter future.

As he disappeared into the depths of the county, one question echoed in the recesses of Solace's mind: Could he ever truly find solace from the demons that lurked in the shadows? The answer remained uncertain, suspended in the delicate balance between justice and the unyielding pursuit of those he had once called brethren. Again, Walter's words creased through his head.

*"You'll never truly escape us, Templar. We will find you."*

## CHAPTER 5

### Striking Gold

T HE STALE ODOR OF BEER AND sweat hung heavy in the air, swirling through the dull tavern. Detective Inspector Shepherd and Sergeant Brown, scanned the crowded room with their raiding eyes. The cops knew they had ventured into the heart of a place where secrets thrived and danger lurked. The cacophony of raucous laughter and clinking glasses filled their ears, drowning out any hope of discreet conversation.

The information that had led them here was like a thread in the labyrinth of their investigation. Barkley Owen—a man with black hair and a distinctive left-handedness—had emerged as their first tangible suspect. A lumberman by profession, Owen seemed to vanish into thin air whenever the authorities got close. But now, armed with a lead, Shepherd and Brown were determined to close in.

The flickering neon lights cast a garish glow on the faces of the patrons, painting them in shades of desperation and hidden motives. Shepherd's gaze settled on a hunched figure seated at the far end of the bar, nursing a drink. The man's unkempt hair fell over his eyes, casting a veil of mystery over his features. The scent of damp wood and fresh sawdust clung to him, a lingering reminder of his trade.

"That's him," Shepherd whispered to Brown, his voice barely audible above the clamor. "Let's move in!" When the Detective made to move, he grabbed him back and whispered again. "Be ready for anything."

As they approached, Owen's eyes darted around the room, his fingers gripping the rim of his glass with a mixture of unease and determination. Sensing the presence of the law, he bolted from his seat, pushing through the crowd with surprising agility. Shepherd and Brown exchanged a glance, their chase beginning in earnest.

The maze of narrow streets seemed to close in on them as they pursued Owen through the labyrinthine town. His silhouette danced in the dim light, disappearing around corners and down alleyways. The scent of damp concrete and old garbage filled their nostrils, an unwelcome companion in their pursuit.

Each step brought them closer, their breaths mingling with the sounds of their pounding footsteps. Owen's figure loomed ahead, a tantalizing glimpse of justice just out of reach. The chase led them to a desolate industrial area, where abandoned warehouses stood like sentinels, their broken windows reflecting shards of moonlight.

Shepherd's heart pounded in his chest as he caught sight of Owen disappearing into one of the dilapidated structures. He motioned for Brown to follow, their senses heightened, and their hands gripping their sidearms. The stale air inside the warehouse clung to their skin, mingling with the scent of rust and decay.

The beam of Shepherd's flashlight cut through the darkness, casting eerie shadows that danced on the peeling walls. The creak of a door and the shuffle of footsteps sent a shiver down their spines. Their hearts raced in unison, the rhythm of their pursuit echoing through the vast emptiness.

"Stop right there, Owen!" Shepherd's voice boomed, its authority commanding the stillness of the space. "You have nowhere left to run."

Owen's figure materialized in the faint glow of the flashlight beam, his eyes wild with desperation. "You'll never catch me!" he spat, his voice laced with defiance.

Shepherd moved forward, his gaze fixed on Owen. "Give it up, Owen. We have evidence, witnesses, and the weight of the law on our side. It's over."

A twisted smile curled on Owen's lips, his body tense with defiance. "You think you can take me down? You have no idea what's at stake here!"

The tension in the air was palpable, a clash of wills that threatened to shatter the fragile. Owen might pull stunts, both detectives suspected so. Every bad guy would.

The air crackled with anticipation as Shepherd and Brown closed the distance between them and Owen. The space seemed to constrict around them, suffocating them with the weight of the impending confrontation. Owen's eyes flickered with a mixture of fear and determination, and his hand slid into his coat pocket, causing Shepherd's heart to skip a beat.

*A gun?*

With a sudden, explosive motion, Owen lunged forward, producing a gleaming switchblade from his pocket. The blade glinted malevolently in the flashlight's beam as he slashed it toward Shepherd, who instinctively ducked and countered with a swift kick to Owen's midsection. The blow knocked the wind out of him, causing him to stagger backward, momentarily disarmed.

Brown, not one to be caught off guard, seized the opportunity and lunged at Owen from the side. His powerful fists swung through the air, connecting with Owen's jaw and sending him sprawling to the ground. But the fight was far from over. Owen sprang back to his feet with a vengeance, his eyes blazing with a rage that matched his unkempt appearance.

The detectives circled Owen cautiously, their movements measured and precise. Shepherd's mind raced, analyzing the fight as it unfolded. He anticipated Owen's next move and parried a series of punches with expert precision. Brown, his brawny frame a formidable presence, engaged in a fierce struggle, grappling with Owen, each determined to gain the upper hand.

The warehouse became a battleground, the sounds of grunts, thuds, and the clash of bodies reverberating through the empty space. Shepherd's fist connected with Owen's jaw, eliciting a pained grunt, while Brown executed a swift knee strike to Owen's abdomen, forcing him to double over in agony.

But Owen, fueled by desperation, fought back with an uncanny resilience. He fought dirty, resorting to biting and scratching, trying to break free from their grip.

He's a berserker!

The detectives struggled to maintain their hold, their determination matched by Owen's unwavering determination to escape justice.

Finally, Shepherd seized an opportunity. As Owen lunged forward, Shepherd sidestepped and expertly executed a sweeping leg kick, knocking Owen off balance.

Brown, quick to capitalize on the opening, delivered a crushing blow to Owen's jaw, sending him sprawling to the ground in a daze.

With their suspect finally subdued, Shepherd and Brown wasted no time. They swiftly handcuffed Owen, ensuring he could no longer pose a threat.

Detective Brown cemented the defeat by pointing a gun to his head. "I'll paint the walls with your blood, asshole!" he said, panting heavily.

The fight had taken its toll on them, their breaths ragged and their bodies marked with bruises and sweat-soaked clothing. But their mission was accomplished.

The two detectives exchanged a glance, a mix of exhaustion and triumph mirrored in their eyes. They knew their relentless pursuit had paid off, and justice would finally be served. Together, they led Owen out of the warehouse, his steps faltering under the weight of defeat.

"Fuck you, idiots. Let me go!" Owen cursed, the corner of his lips etched with pasta of blood, sweat and dirt.

As they emerged into the dim light of the night, the cacophony of the city's sounds enveloped them once more. Shepherd and Brown shared a silent understanding, knowing that this victory was not just for them but for the countless victims whose lives had been shattered by Owen's actions.

With Owen in custody, they made their way to their awaiting police vehicle, ready to bring him to justice and close this chapter of their investigation. The weight of the night's events pressed upon them, but they walked with heads held high, knowing they had upheld the law in the face of danger and uncertainty.

# CHAPTER 6

## One More Down

T HE MURDER AT OLIVE train station was only the first of many more to come. That Friday night, the media gathered again for another newsgathering feast at the

Olive Boulevard train station.

Same place.

Same platform.

Same bridge.

Same time.

Detective Inspector Shepherd stood at the edge of the crime scene, his eyes narrowed as he took in the grim sight before him. The morning mist lingered around Olive Boulevard train station, cloaking it in an eerie atmosphere.

The yellow police tape fluttered in the wind, marking the boundaries of yet another brutal murder.

Caden Stones lay sprawled on the ground, his once robust frame now lifeless. The pot bellied lumberman had met the same fate as Detective Inspector Hine, his throat slashed with ruthless precision. A crimson pool spread beneath him, mirroring the sky's crimson hues as dawn approached.

Shepherd's heart sank. The pattern was unmistakable—a serial killer was on the loose, leaving behind a trail of death and fear. It was a chilling realization that sent a shiver down his spine.

He stepped closer to the body, carefully avoiding the bloodstains. The scent of death lingered in the air, a sickening mix of copper and decay. As he bent down, he couldn't help but notice the texture of the wounds, the way the flesh had been ruthlessly sliced. The killer was methodical, skilled—a predator hidden in the shadows.

*A damn merciless murderer!*

"DI Shepherd," a voice called from behind, snapping him out of his thoughts.

Shepherd turned to find Detective Inspector Collins, a seasoned officer with graying hair, approaching with a grave expression on his face. Collins had been Shepherd's mentor during his early years in the force, a mentor whose wisdom and guidance had shaped him into the detective he was today.

"Collins," Shepherd greeted, his voice tinged with a mixture of concern and determination. "It's the same as Hine, isn't it?"

Collins nodded grimly. "The M.O. is identical. This is the work of a meticulous killer, Shepherd—a predator who revels in darkness. We need to catch them before they strike again."

Shepherd's eyes scanned the area, his mind racing to make sense of the puzzle before him. He knew that to catch this killer, he needed to understand them, to think like them. The answers lay in the details, in the sensations that surrounded the crime scene.

He crouched down beside Stones, his gloved hand gingerly reaching out to touch the cold skin. He felt a sudden surge of anger, mingled with determination. The killer had taken another life, leaving behind shattered families and a city gripped by fear. Shepherd refused to let this continue.

As he rose to his feet, Shepherd's gaze fell upon a shadowy figure lurking in the distance. It was a silhouette, barely visible against the backdrop of the mist-covered station. The figure seemed out of place—a dark anomaly amidst the morning light.

"Collins, do you see that?" Shepherd pointed, his voice tense.

Collins squinted, following Shepherd's gaze. "I see it, Shepherd." Before he could complete his next statement, Shepherd was on the move.

Together, they moved cautiously towards the shadowy figure, their footsteps muffled by the silence of the station. The air grew thick with anticipation as they closed the distance, their hearts pounding in unison.

"Stop right there!" Shepherd commanded, his voice cutting through the stillness.

The figure froze, slowly turning to face the detectives. It was a woman, her eyes wide with fear. Her pale face was streaked with tears, mirroring the anguish of a grieving city.

"Please, don't hurt me," she whimpered, her voice trembling. "I saw him—I saw the killer!"

Shepherd and Collins exchanged glances, their senses heightened. This woman could be their key to unlocking the secrets of the killer's identity.

"Tell us everything," Shepherd urged, his voice steady.

The woman took a deep breath, attempting to compose herself as she recounted her chilling encounter.

"I was waiting for the train," she began, her voice shaky. "I saw a man lurking in the shadows near the platform. He was tall, wearing a dark coat, and his eyes... they were cold, like a predator's."

She paused, her hands trembling, as she relived the fear that had coursed through her veins. Shepherd leaned in, his gaze unwavering, urging her to continue.

"I could smell him," she continued, her voice barely above a whisper. "There was a faint, metallic scent, like blood. I tried to ignore it, but it lingered, tainting the air around him."

Shepherd's mind raced, connecting the dots between her description and the details of the crime scenes. The scent of blood was a crucial clue—a signature left by the killer, perhaps unconsciously.

"Did you see him do anything?" Collins interjected, his eyes locked on the woman.

"He... he was holding something," she stammered. "It looked like a knife—a gleaming blade catching the faint glow of the streetlights. He... he disappeared into the shadows before I could do anything."

Shepherd's jaw clenched, his mind piecing together the fragments of information. The killer was meticulous, leaving behind no trace but instilling a sense of fear in those who encountered him. They needed more—more witnesses, more evidence—to bring this monster to justice.

Immediately, the homeless man's account crept into Detective Shepherd's head. He once believed everything he said and ended up chasing a blind lead. Now, he had issues believing the woman before him even though he'd never tell her he doesn't believe her.

His eyes off his notepad, he stared at the woman, studying her more intensely this time. "Are you sure about all you've just said?"

The woman sneered. "I'm 48. I wouldn't be lying to the Police for crying out loud," she nagged.

"Come on. That's alright," Collins chipped in. "We believe your account, Mrs Baker."

"Thank you," Shepherd said, his voice laced with gratitude. "You've provided us with valuable information. We will do everything in our power to stop him. Apologies if I sounded offensive."

The woman nodded, tears still streaming down her face, as Shepherd and Collins turned their attention back to the crime scene. The sun had risen, casting a faint glow over the station, but the air was heavy with an unshakeable dread.

"We need to gather more witness statements," Shepherd declared. "We can't let this killer continue to strike in the shadows."

Collins nodded in agreement. "We'll mobilize the team, talk to everyone who was at the station this morning. We need to find anyone who saw something, smelled something... anything that could help us catch this monster."

As they walked back toward the station entrance, Shepherd's phone buzzed in his pocket. He pulled it out, seeing a text message from the forensic team. The message contained a photograph—an image of a small, intricately designed symbol etched into the victim's wrist.

Shepherd's heart skipped a beat. The symbol was hauntingly familiar—a symbol he had seen before. It was a connection, a link that brought back memories of a past case—one that had remained unsolved.

"This... this can't be a coincidence," Shepherd muttered, his voice filled with disbelief. "Collins, we need to talk."

*** 

The dots were slowly coming together but Detective Shepherd just couldn't get a clear picture of it. He felt it but could wrap his head around it. He was too tense to let it align.

Leaning against the unpainted dirty wall, Detective Collins frowned, sensing the urgency in Shepherd's tone. They found a secluded spot away from prying eyes, and

Shepherd relayed his revelation—the symbol, the resemblance to a previous case.

Collins listened intently, his expression darkening with each passing word. "If this is true, Shepherd, it means we're dealing with something far more sinister than we could have imagined."

Shepherd nodded, his gaze fixed on the distant horizon. "We need to dig deeper, Collins. Unearth the truth behind these symbols, behind the past. There's more to this case than meets the eye."

As they parted ways, Shepherd felt a surge of determination coursing through his veins. He knew they were running out of time—each murder brought them closer to another victim, to another grieving family. The shadow of the serial killer loomed over the city, suffocating its inhabitants with fear.

But Detective Inspector Shepherd refused to succumb to fear. He had faced darkness before, and he had emerged victorious. This case would be no different. No way.

Shepherd returned to his office, a realm of organized chaos, filled with whiteboards covered in photographs, notes, and red strings connecting pieces of the puzzle. It was his tiny world—fledged with scattered clues yet unanswered questions and unsolved mental and investigative puzzles.

With tiredness in his limbs, he slumped into his desk, staring at the symbol on his phone, delving into the depths of his memory.

Memories of a cold, desolate night, where the stench of death had hung in the air. A night where a similar symbol had marked the crime scene—a symbol that had haunted Shepherd's dreams for years. A case that had gone unsolved, its secrets buried beneath layers of time.

As he further stared into the picture, the memories of it began flooding his head in fragments. Lastly, the dots connected.

*Obsidian Order.*

That was the word he had been looking for. The same word he heard in his dream some twice in one night. The symbol held a close resemblance to what he saw within the chambers of the secret organization.

He reached for the file of the old case, its cover worn with age, and opened it to reveal a trove of photographs, witness statements, and reports. Shepherd dove into the contents, immersing himself in the darkness of the past, searching for the missing pieces that connected the dots.

As he read, a sense of unease washed over him. The similarities were uncanny—both cases involved meticulous killings, the distinctive symbol, and an air of mystery that shrouded the culprits. The old case had slipped through their fingers, the truth eluding them. But now, fate had brought Shepherd face to face with the same evil, demanding justice.

Time seemed to blur as Shepherd delved deeper into the files, his fingers tracing the outlines of the photographs. He scrutinized the details, absorbing the sights, the smells, the textures, desperate to uncover the truth.

The door to his office creaked open, interrupting his thoughts. Detective Brown stepped inside, his face etched with concern. "We have something. A witness you might want to meet," he announced.

"Anything tangible?" Shepherd asked, desperation clearly spelt on his glassy eyeballs.

"Apparently. There's claims of seeing the killer near the previous crime scene."

Shepherd's heart quickened. "Bring him in. We can't afford to let any lead slip away."

Brown chuckled a bit before stepping out. "It's a she!"

Minutes later, a young woman entered the room. Her eyes held a mixture of fear and determination as she faced the detectives. She had seen the killer, witnessed the darkness firsthand. She is blonde and thin. As she spoke and kept swinging her head , her burgundy-brown hair swung sideways in an uneven rhythm.

"I smelled him," she confessed, her voice barely above a whisper. "A sickly sweet scent, like rotting flowers. It made me nauseous."

Shepherd's mind raced, drawing a connection to the metallic scent described by the previous witness. Two distinct smells, two different crimes, but both tied to the same killer.

*Mysterious!*

"Did you see anything else?" Collins inquired, his gaze fixed on the young woman. He was back in the office. Detective Shepherd thought he had left. He felt slightly relieved that an officer he held at high esteem is dearly interested in helping him to the roots of the investigation.

"He wore a ring," she said, her voice quivering. "A silver ring with an engraved symbol—a symbol that chilled me to the bone."

Shepherd's heart skipped a beat. The symbol—the engraved ring—was all too familiar. The pieces of the puzzle were coming together, revealing a malevolent force hidden in plain sight.

"We're close, Collins," Shepherd declared, his voice filled with resolve. "We're on the verge of unraveling the truth. We just need one more lead."

Collins nodded, his eyes reflecting the same determination. "Let's find that lead, Shepherd. Let's bring this monster to justice."

As they prepared to leave the office, Shepherd's phone buzzed once again. He glanced at the screen, a new message illuminating the display. The message was short, but it sent a chill down his spine:

*"Time befriends no one, Detective Shepherd. It is on the run. It never stops."*

Shepherd's grip tightened around the phone, his mind racing. The killer knew. They knew that the detectives were closing in, that the shadows were receding, revealing their true face.

A sense of urgency surged within Shepherd as he exchanged a glance with Collins. The race against time had intensified, the stakes higher than ever. The killer's taunting message only fueled Shepherd's determination. They had to act swiftly to prevent another life from being claimed.

Shepherd and Collins rushed back to the station, their minds focused on finding the elusive lead that would bring them face to face with the killer. The atmosphere at Olive Boulevard train station had changed. An air of unease now permeated the surroundings, as if the very walls whispered secrets and concealed danger.

They combed through the crowd, speaking to witnesses, searching for anyone who might hold a crucial piece of information. The scent of anticipation mingled with the station's usual odors—the metallic tang of train tracks, the distant aroma of coffee, and the faint hint of diesel fuel.

Then, amidst the crowd, Shepherd's attention was drawn to a young man. His eyes darted nervously, avoiding contact with the detectives. Something about him seemed out of place—furtive, on edge.

Shepherd approached the man cautiously, his senses heightened. "Excuse me, sir. Can we have a word?"

The man's eyes flickered with a mix of fear and guilt as he stammered, "I... I don't know anything."

Shepherd leaned closer, his voice low but commanding. "Don't lie to me. We can sense when someone's hiding something. Speak the truth, and it might save lives."

The young man hesitated, his eyes shifting from Shepherd to Collins. Beads of sweat formed on his brow, betraying his nervousness.

"Come on," Collins said, turning in Shepherd's direction. "No one's implicating you. Just go ahead. Tell us what you know or perhaps saw! We'll protect you."

"Isn't that what all cops say," the man hushed, looking away with utter disinterest.

Detective Shepherd pulled his badge and flashed it before the man. "Detective Inspector Shepherd George! I pledge to keep you under the radar!"

"I... I saw something," he finally admitted, his voice trembling.

"Where?" Detective Collins chipped in. "Late at night, when the station was almost empty. I saw a man— dark coat, cold eyes. He... he had a distinctive smell. Like burning wood and sulfur."

Shepherd's heart skipped a beat. The description matched the previous witness accounts—an intricate web of senses connecting each crime scene, each encounter with the killer.

"Tell us everything," Collins urged, his voice gentle but firm.

The young man nodded, recounting the harrowing sight he had witnessed. "He was near the platform, holding a knife. He... he carved something into the wall, a symbol. Then he disappeared into the darkness."

Shepherd's mind raced, piecing together the information. The symbol, the scent, the chilling presence— it all aligned with their investigation. They were closing in, unraveling the sinister tapestry spun by the serial killer.

"We need to find that symbol," Shepherd said, his voice resolute. "It's the key to this puzzle, the doorway to the truth."

They retraced the young man's steps, arriving at the desolate part of the platform where he had witnessed the killer's act. Shepherd's eyes scanned the walls, searching for the engraved symbol that had haunted their investigations.

Then, in the dim light, Shepherd's gaze fell upon it—an intricate, twisted symbol etched into the cold concrete. Its presence sent shivers down his spine, the weight of its meaning pressing upon him.

"This is it," Shepherd murmured, his voice laced with a mix of anticipation and apprehension. "The symbol that links the past to the present, the gateway to the killer's identity."

But as Shepherd took a step closer to examine the symbol, a sharp gust of wind swept through the station. In the fleeting darkness, a figure emerged—a silhouette cloaked in mystery, standing just beyond the reach of the dim lights.

Shepherd's heart raced, a chill crawling up his spine. "Collins, look!"

Collins turned, his eyes widening in disbelief. "It can't be..."

The figure's cold, calculating eyes locked with Shepherd's. A wicked smile played upon their lips, a taunting challenge in their gaze. They vanished into the shadows, leaving behind an eerie silence that echoed through the station. Shepherd's instincts kicked into overdrive, his heart pounding with a mix of adrenaline and a burning desire for justice.

"Collins, we can't let them escape again!" Shepherd shouted, his voice filled with determination.

They chased after the figure, their footsteps echoing through the station, as they navigated the labyrinthine corridors, desperate to catch a glimpse of the elusive killer. But the station seemed to conspire against them, concealing the perpetrator's every move.

As they reached a dimly lit platform, Shepherd's senses heightened. A pungent scent filled the air, a cocktail of dampness and decay, intertwining with the metallic stench of blood. It was a tangible reminder that they were on the trail of a predator who was revealed in darkness.

Their footsteps echoed in synchrony, a rhythmic beat urging them forward. Shepherd's eyes scanned the surroundings, searching for any sign of the killer. Then, in the corner of his vision, a flicker of movement—a shadow blending seamlessly with the darkness.

He lunged forward, fueled by determination, his fingers grazing fabric, but it slipped through his grasp like smoke. The killer was swift, leaving behind only the trace of their presence, a lingering enigma.

Collins caught up, gasping for breath, his voice laced with frustration. "They're always one step ahead!"

Shepherd's gaze remained fixed on the spot where the killer had stood. "We need to regroup, Collins. Gather the team. We can't let them escape again."

Collins nodded, his eyes mirroring Shepherd's unwavering resolve. They would not let the trail grow cold, not again.

***

They are back to the drawing board again. Shepherd assembled the team, sharing the new information they had gathered—the witnesses' accounts, the symbol, the distinct smells. The room buzzed with a sense of urgency and shared determination.

"We're facing a cunning adversary," Shepherd addressed his team. "But we have one thing they don't—the power of collaboration, the strength of our unity. We will leave no stone unturned, no clue unexamined. We will bring this killer to justice."

Days turned into nights, as the investigation intensified. They chased leads, analyzed evidence, and pursued every possible angle. The city trembled beneath the weight of anticipation, each passing day inching them closer to the truth.

Then, amidst the chaos of the investigation, Shepherd received an anonymous package—a worn leather journal. Its pages whispered secrets, promising revelations that could unravel the twisted tapestry woven by the killer.

As Shepherd flipped through the pages, he stumbled upon an entry—a chilling revelation that sent shivers down his spine. The entry described a series of murders, meticulously planned, each victim marked by the same symbol. It was a dark chronicle, a testament to the killer's depravity.

But as Shepherd delved deeper into the journal, searching for a clue that would unmask the killer's identity, he realized the final pages were missing. A sense of frustration and urgency gripped him. They were running out of time.

Shepherd knew he had to confront the killer, to bring an end to the reign of terror that plagued the city. The final confrontation loomed before him, a battle of wits and determination.

With the missing pages as their guide, Shepherd and his team pieced together a pattern—an intricate web of connections, leading them to a forsaken warehouse on the outskirts of the city.

*It's time to get down!*

\*\*\*

The air is stuffy. As they approached the warehouse, darkness engulfing its decaying structure, Shepherd's heart pounded in his chest. The smell of impending danger hung heavy in the air. Every step brought them closer to the answers they sought, closer to the heart of darkness.

With weapons drawn and hearts racing, Shepherd and his team cautiously entered the warehouse. The flickering light of their flashlights pierced through the gloom, revealing a labyrinth of forgotten crates and discarded remnants of a forgotten era.

The atmosphere was suffocating, filled with the scent of dampness and decay. The air hung heavy with anticipation, as if the warehouse itself held its breath, aware of the impending confrontation.

They followed the trail of clues, their senses heightened, every creaking floorboard, every rustling sound setting their nerves on edge. The killer's presence loomed in the shadows, a malevolent force waiting to strike.

Suddenly, a voice, cold and calculated, pierced the silence. "Impressive, Detective Shepherd. You've come so far, but it ends here."

Shepherd's grip tightened around his weapon as he directed his flashlight towards the source of the voice. A figure emerged from the darkness, their face obscured, a chilling smile etched upon their lips.

"We've danced this dance before," the figure continued, his voice a haunting melody. "But this time, I won't be caught."

Shepherd's voice was steady, his resolve unyielding. "Your reign of terror ends tonight. Your victims will find justice."

In a swift motion, the masked built-like-a-brick-house lunged forward, launching himself into a violent assault. A battle ensued, a symphony of punches, dodges, and desperate gasps for breath. The warehouse reverberated with the sounds of struggle and pain.

Amidst the chaos, Shepherd caught a glimpse of the figure's face after pulling his mask aside—a twisted visage, eyes filled with a sickening blend of amusement and malevolence. The adrenaline surged through Shepherd's veins, heightening his senses. He could almost taste victory, a taste tinged with the metallic tang of blood.

But the figure was cunning, slipping through his defenses with the agility of a predator. His movements were fluid, calculated, as if he had anticipated every countermove. Shepherd knew he was up against a formidable adversary—one who had honed their skills through each meticulously planned murder.

As the battle raged on, Shepherd's mind raced. He analyzed the future's style,his patterns, searching for a weakness, a moment of vulnerability. And then, it clicked—his reliance on the element of surprise.

With a surge of adrenaline, Shepherd evaded a blow and seized the opportunity. He launched himself forward, tackling him to the ground, their bodies colliding with a resounding thud.

The man's eyes widened in shock, their facade of confidence crumbling. "How... How did you..."

Shepherd pressed his advantage, his voice laced with determination. "You underestimated the power of justice, the strength of those who fight against the darkness. Your reign of terror ends now."

As Shepherd's team closed in, the figure's expression shifted from defiance to desperation. He knew his time was running out, that the walls were closing in.

But just as victory seemed within reach, a deafening explosion shook the warehouse. Flames erupted, devouring the darkness, engulfing everything in their path. Chaos and panic ensued as Shepherd and his incoming team fought against the consuming inferno.

In the midst of the chaos, the figure vanished into the smoke, leaving Shepherd with a bitter taste of both triumph and frustration. The battle had been won, but the war was not yet over.

As the flames roared and the warehouse crumbled, Shepherd emerged from the inferno, his eyes scanning the wreckage, searching for any trace of the figure. But he had disappeared, leaving behind only ashes and unanswered questions.

Detective Inspector Shepherd stood amidst the ruins, a mixture of relief and uncertainty washing over him. The pursuit of justice would continue, the hunt for the elusive killer would persist.

With the smoke still billowing around him, Shepherd knew that the investigation was far from over. The figure who might perhaps be the killer had slipped through their fingers once again, leaving behind a trail of destruction and unanswered questions.

.

As the fire brigade arrived to contain the blaze, Shepherd's mind raced with possibilities. How had the killer managed to escape amidst the chaos? And more importantly, what was their next move?

Shepherd turned to his team, their faces etched with exhaustion and determination. "We can't let this setback discourage us. We've come too far to give up now. We need to regroup, reassess our evidence, and find any lead that could bring us closer to capturing the killer."

Brown nodded, his voice filled with conviction. "We'll leave no stone unturned, Shepherd. We'll analyze every piece of evidence, revisit every witness statement. We won't rest until justice is served."

With renewed determination, Shepherd and his team set to work. They sifted through the charred remains of the warehouse, salvaging any clues that might have survived the inferno. The acrid scent of smoke lingered in the air, a constant reminder of the figure's escape.

Days turned into weeks as they meticulously reconstructed the events leading up to the warehouse confrontation. They pored over every detail, analyzing the journal, re-examining witness testimonies, and re-tracing the killer's steps. It was a race against time, as they knew the killer wouldn't remain dormant for long.

Then, amidst the mountain of evidence, Shepherd's eyes fell upon a small, overlooked detail—a photo, partially licked by the fire. It depicted the figure, his face partially obscured, but Shepherd recognized the distinct glint of determination in their eyes. He saw it. He couldn't miss to recognize it.

He called Collins over, excitement coursing through his veins. "Look at this, Collins. It's a photo of him."

"You saw his face?"

"A part of it. His eyes ring a bell."

Collins examined the photo closely, his eyes widening with recognition. "Shepherd, I've seen this person before. They were at the station during Detective Hine's murder. They were watching, observing."

Shepherd's heart raced. "That's it, Collins! We have a connection between the victims and the killer. We need to find out who this person is, their motive, their identity."

The team mobilized, delving deeper into the lives of the victims, searching for any potential links to the enigmatic figure in the photo. They reached out to family, friends, and acquaintances, desperate for any information that could shed light on the killer's identity.

Another week faded as the investigation intensified. Shepherd's mind became consumed with thoughts of the killer, their methods, their next move. The county held its breath, wary of the lurking darkness that had claimed the lives of Detective Hine and Caden Stones.

And then, in the midst of the relentless pursuit, Shepherd received yet another chilling message—an anonymous note left on his desk at the precinct. It was brief, but its words sent a shiver down his spine:

"Time befriends no one, Detective Shepherd. It is on the run. It never stops."

Shepherd's heart pounded with a mix of anticipation and trepidation. The killer had resurfaced, taunting him, challenging him to a deadly game of cat and mouse. With every passing moment, the stakes grew higher, the need to capture the killer more urgent.

As Shepherd readied himself for the inevitable showdown, he knew that the fate of not only the city but also his own life hung in the balance.

The clock was ticking, and time was running out.

## CHAPTER 7

### Busted!

T HE FULLY LIT INTERROGATION room in the Sumter County Police Department's station was suffused with tension. Detective Inspector Shepherd leaned against the cold metal table, his gaze fixed on Barkley Owen, the prime suspect in the murder of Detective Hine. Barkley, a rugged man with unkempt hair and a weary look in his eyes, sat on the opposite side of the table, his hands clenched tightly.

The heavy silence was broken by the squeak of the door as Sheriff Thompson entered, his authoritative presence filling the room. His sharp eyes surveyed the scene before settling on Barkley. "Mr. Owen," he said in a deep baritone, "we have some questions for you."

Barkley's eyes flickered with a mix of fear and determination as he locked eyes with the sheriff. "I can't respond to your questions!" Owen barked.

"We can assign you an attorney if that's what you want," Detective Shepherd chipped him, showing more interest in the interrogation like never before.

Owen banged the table loudly. "I do not need a lawyer to speak for me."

Detective Shepherd signaled Sheriff Thompson to excuse them and then turned to Owen. "What do you want, Owen?"

I've already told you everything I know," he replied, his voice tinged with exhaustion. "I didn't kill Detective Hine."

"Why did you run upon sighting us at the tavern?" Detective Shepherd asked.

Owen didn't respond. He kept mute.

Detective Shepherd, known for his keen sense of observation, studied Barkley intently. He noticed the wear and tear on his clothes, the dirt under his fingernails, and the faint scent of desperation that hung in the air. Something about Barkley's story didn't quite fit, but the detective couldn't ignore the niggling doubt that plagued his mind.

"I find it hard to believe," Detective Shepherd interjected, his voice steady and unwavering. "You ran away when the police first came for you. Why?"

Barkley's eyes darted around the room, searching for an escape from the mounting pressure. "My house was up for foreclosure," he admitted, his voice strained. "I couldn't bear to leave my belongings behind. I had nowhere to take them."

Detective Shepherd's brow furrowed, his mind grappling with the conflicting pieces of the puzzle. He leaned forward, his voice low and probing. "Tell me, Mr. Owen, where were you at the time of Detective Hine's murder?"

A flicker of relief passed over Barkley's face as he answered, "I was at the abandoned café on Maple Street. It's where I go to clear my head, to escape the chaos of my life."

At Detective Shepherd's signal, Sheriff Thompson was back. Shepherd's eyes narrowed, a glimmer of hope emerging from the depths of doubt. "Sheriff, I want you to check his alibi. Thoroughly," he commanded, his voice tinged with urgency.

*"If Barkley is telling the truth, then we've been chasing the wrong man."*

Sheriff Thompson nodded solemnly, his gaze shifting from Barkley to Detective Shepherd. "I'll have my deputies investigate the café and confirm his whereabouts," he assured, his voice carrying the weight of determination.

As the room fell into silence once again, Detective Shepherd's mind churned with the possibility that they had indeed been barking up the wrong tree. The smell of anxiety hung in the air, intermingling with the acrid scent of stale coffee that permeated the room. He couldn't shake the feeling that something crucial was eluding him, like pieces of a jigsaw puzzle scattered across the table.

For agonizing minutes as they awaited the sheriff's update. The tension in the room was palpable, each passing second stretching their patience thin. Finally, the door creaked open, and Sheriff Thompson strode in, a sense of urgency etched across his face.

"Barkley's alibi checks out," he announced, his voice laden with a mix of surprise and disbelief. "Multiple witnesses saw him at the café during the time of the murder."

Detective Shepherd's heart pounded in his chest as he absorbed the revelation. The weight of certainty lifted from his shoulders, leaving behind a void filled with more questions than answers. The realization that they had been pursuing an innocent man shook the foundation of Detective Shepherd's beliefs.

Barkley, released on bail, stood before Detective Shepherd and Sheriff Thompson, a mixture of relief and frustration evident in his eyes. "I told you I didn't do it," he muttered, his voice tinged with bitterness. "But nobody wanted to listen."

Detective Shepherd, his mind still reeling from the revelation, stepped forward, a deep sense of regret tugging at his conscience. "I'm sorry," he began, his voice laden with sincerity. "We were convinced you were the culprit. But we made a mistake."

Barkley's gaze bore into Detective Shepherd's, the weariness in his eyes replaced by a glimmer of defiance. "Mistakes can cost lives," he replied, his voice laced with an edge of anger. "You have no idea what this has done to me."

A heavy silence settled over the room, broken only by the distant hum of the police station. Detective Shepherd knew he couldn't undo the damage that had been done, the relentless pursuit of an innocent man. But he vowed to make it right, to find the true killer and bring them to justice.

"Please understand," Detective Shepherd implored, his voice softening. "We'll find the person responsible for

Detective Hine's murder. And we'll do everything in our power to make it right."

Barkley's gaze wavered for a moment, his anger giving way to a glimmer of hope. "You'd better," he muttered, his voice barely audible. "Because I won't rest until the truth is revealed."

More than anything he's ever been committed to, Detective Shepherd delved deeper into the investigation, haunted by the realization that they had wasted valuable time pursuing an innocent man. The sights and sounds of the crime scene played on a loop in his mind, the scent of blood and fear lingering in his nostrils.

The investigation led him down a twisted path, each piece of evidence unveiling a new layer of deception and intrigue. The shadows of doubt that had plagued him before now morphed into an all-consuming darkness, threatening to consume his resolve.

But Detective Shepherd refused to falter. With each step, he could feel the weight of the truth inching closer, propelled by a relentless determination to redeem himself and find justice for Detective Hine.

In the dead of night, as rain pounded against the windows of his office, Detective Shepherd poured over the case files, his eyes scanning the words, searching for a hidden clue. The air was heavy with the smell of wet pavement, and the rhythmic tapping of raindrops against the glass served as a constant reminder of the task at hand.

Suddenly, a photograph caught his attention—a seemingly insignificant detail that had eluded him before. He reached out, his fingers trembling as he traced the outline of a face, a face that shouldn't have been there.

A gasp escaped his lips as the realization hit him like a lightning bolt. The puzzle pieces were finally falling into place, and the true magnitude of the conspiracy began to unravel before his eyes. Detective Shepherd knew that he was onto something big, something that could shatter everything they thought they knew.

With a renewed sense of purpose, Detective Shepherd snatched his coat from the hanger, determined to confront the shadowy figures that had evaded his grasp. The echoes of his footsteps reverberated through the empty police station as he made his way to the exit.

As he stepped into the rain-soaked night, Detective Shepherd couldn't help but wonder if he was ready for what awaited him. The line between right and wrong had blurred, and he found himself standing on the precipice of a truth that could destroy everything he held dear.

The county streets glistened under the dim glow of streetlights, raindrops cascading down like tears from the heavens. Detective Shepherd's senses heightened, every sound and movement around him amplified in the silence of the night. The scent of wet asphalt mingled with the electricity in the air, adding to the sense of anticipation that coursed through his veins.

He had a hunch, an instinct that led him to a destination he couldn't ignore—the abandoned warehouse on the outskirts of town. It was a place whispered about in the darkest corners of the city, a hub for illicit activities and the meeting point of shadows. If there was anyone with the answers he sought, it would be there.

*What are you doing, Shepherd?*

As he approached the desolate building, its decaying façade loomed like a monolith in the darkness. Detective Shepherd's heart raced with a blend of apprehension and adrenaline, his hand instinctively resting on his holstered gun. He knew he was about to face dangerous individuals, ones who would stop at nothing to protect their secrets.

With a steady breath, Detective Shepherd pushed open the rusted door, the creaking sound echoing through the cavernous space. His eyes adjusted to the dim light that seeped through broken windows, revealing the remnants of a forgotten past—a tattered couch, discarded syringes, and graffiti adorning the walls like cryptic messages.

The faint sound of murmurs reached his ears, drawing him deeper into the warehouse's depths. He moved stealthily, his steps guided by shadows, his senses attuned to every sound and movement. The air was heavy with anticipation, the taste of danger lingering on his tongue.

Finally, he reached the heart of the warehouse, where a circle of figures stood, their faces masked by darkness.

The flickering glow of a single, dangling light bulb illuminated their silhouettes, their whispers of conspiracy floating through the air like venomous serpents.

Detective Shepherd stepped into the circle, his voice cutting through the tension. "I know what you've done," he declared, his words a powerful crescendo. "You thought you could hide, but the truth always finds its way to the surface."

The figures turned towards him, their eyes narrowing with a mix of surprise and contempt. A cold silence enveloped the space, broken only by the sound of rain tapping against the warehouse roof. Then, a voice emerged from the darkness, dripping with icy disdain.

"Detective Shepherd," the figure sneered, their voice laced with a hint of amusement. "You underestimate the power of those who control the shadows. You're treading on dangerous ground."

Detective Shepherd locked eyes with the figure, a fire burning in his gaze. "I'm done playing your game," he retorted, his voice resolute. "I won't let innocent lives be sacrificed for your sinister agenda."

As the confrontation escalated, the tension in the warehouse thickened, the air crackling with electricity. Detective Shepherd knew he had reached a pivotal moment—one that could either break the case wide open or push him closer to the edge of his own demise.

Just as he prepared to make his move, a piercing gunshot shattered the stillness. Time seemed to freeze as Detective Shepherd's body jolted backward, pain searing through his chest. The world spun, sounds muffled as he crumpled to the ground, blood staining his shirt.

Through a haze of agony, Detective Shepherd's vision blurred, his mind struggling to comprehend what had just transpired. The figures in the warehouse began to fade, their voices distant echoes. Darkness encroached around him, threatening to swallow him whole.

With his last ounce of strength, Detective Shepherd reached into his pocket and fumbled for his phone, desperately dialing a familiar number, praying that help would arrive in time. The line rang once, twice, before a voice on the other end answered.

"Detective Shepherd? What's the situation?"

It was Detective Brown, the stalwart ally who had stood by him throughout the investigation. The detective's voice trembled with pain as he choked out the words, "Warehouse. Pincord Street... send backup."

The detective's voice crackled with urgency. "Hang in there. On our way!"

Detective Shepherd's body grew weaker with each passing moment, the pain intensifying. He could hear sirens wailing in the distance, growing louder, promising salvation. Yet, darkness encroached upon his vision, threatening to claim him before the cavalry arrived.

As he lay there, the smell of iron mingling with the scent of rain, memories flooded his mind. The faces of the victims he had fought for, the voices of the desperate pleading for justice—all served as a reminder of his purpose, his unwavering commitment to the truth.

A flicker of determination ignited within Detective Shepherd, a refusal to let darkness prevail. With a surge of willpower, he forced his eyes open, a glimmer of light breaking through the abyss. He wouldn't let his pursuit of justice end here, not like this.

The sound of approaching footsteps reverberated through the warehouse, growing louder with each passing second. Sheriff Thompson burst through the door, his deputies following close behind, their guns drawn, ready to face the unknown.

Time seemed to stretch as Detective Brown's gaze fell upon Detective Shepherd, lying battered on the ground. "Shepherd" he cried, his voice thick with concern. "Hold on, help is here."

Paramedics rushed to the detective's side, their skilled hands working swiftly to stabilize him, to keep him from slipping away. But the battle wasn't over yet—there were still answers to uncover, a web of corruption to dismantle.

As the paramedics carried Detective Shepherd out of the warehouse, he clung to the fragments of consciousness, his mind aflame with determination. He couldn't let the truth be silenced, couldn't let the sacrifices made along the way be in vain.

The investigation had taken a dangerous turn, leading him closer to the heart of darkness, where powerful forces conspired to hide their sins. And Detective Shepherd, wounded but unbroken, vowed to return—to uncover the secrets that lay within the shadows and bring those responsible to justice.

The rain continued to fall, washing away the bloodstains from the pavement, as the detective was loaded into the ambulance, his fate uncertain. But one thing was clear: Detective Inspector Shepherd would stop at nothing to see the case through, to unearth the truth that had eluded them all.

And as the ambulance sirens pierced the night, fading into the distance, a new chapter unfolded—one filled with peril, redemption, and a relentless pursuit of justice that would forever change the course of Sumter County's history.

But again, it was another dream.

His eyes dilated in panic, wide Detective Shepherd sprung his frame off the bed, feeling uncomfortable in a pool of his own sweat.

*"You're not dead. It's a dream."*

## CHAPTER 8

### Unloyal Loyalist

S OLACE STARTED FINDING HAPPINESS IN SOLITUDE. Swallowed by the pitch darkness in his room, his mind clouded with uncertainty and doubt. The weight of recent events pressed upon him, and the money that once seemed so enticing now felt tainted, like blood money. He glanced nervously at the stack of bills on the table, the fruits of his loyalty to Walter Tyndale and the criminal organization.

It meant nothing to him anymore. It disgusted him. The sight of it pierced his heart with regrets and angst.

As the news of Detective Hine's murder continued to dominate the headlines, Solace's anxiety grew exponentially. The police and sheriff's department were surely closing in on him, their eyes narrowing, their investigation inching closer to his doorstep. Fear clung to him like a suffocating shroud, leaving him questioning his allegiance to Walter and the organization.

He remembered the night—all of it. He recalled paying the street kid a wad of cash to lure the ever helpful cop right into his den. He recalled the other lady who joined the decoy. Most importantly, he recalled the fearless face of Detective Hine before passing out. He couldn't forget his kicks. His jerks. His curses. His cries.

He had always known that disobedience within their ranks carried dire consequences, but now, faced with the reality of potentially losing his life, Solace couldn't help but question the purpose behind the organization's relentless demands for more bloodshed. Detective Hine's murder had already brought too much attention, too much risk.

On a particularly restless night, as the rain pelted against the windowpane, Solace found himself face-to-face with Walter. The room exuded an atmosphere heavy with tension, the air thick with unsaid words. Solace watched his boss, searching for answers in the depths of Walter's eyes.

"We're walking on thin ice, Solace," Walter began, his voice laced with a mix of warning and concern. "The investigation is closing in, and if they trace it back to us, neither of us will go scot-free."

Solace shifted uneasily, his gaze never wavering from Walter's piercing stare. "Then why are we still taking risks? Why are we still killing?"

Walter's expression hardened, his lips curling into a sinister smile. "There's something you don't understand, Solace. Something you're missing," he replied cryptically. "Trust me, we have our reasons. Trust is what binds us together."

Solace's brow furrowed, his mind racing to decipher the hidden meaning behind Walter's words. But before he could press further, the sound of footsteps echoed from the hallway outside. Both men turned their attention to the door as it swung open, revealing a tall, shadowy figure.

Detective Callahan stepped into the room, his gaze cold and calculating. His arrival sent a chill down Solace's spine, and he could almost taste the bitterness of imminent danger. The detective's eyes narrowed as they locked onto Solace, his voice cutting through the tension-filled silence.

"Templar Solace , you're under arrest for the murder of Detective Hine," Callahan declared, his voice laced with a mixture of triumph and satisfaction. "You won't be able to escape justice this time."

Solace's heart raced in his chest, his senses heightened as adrenaline surged through his veins. He glanced at Walter, his eyes pleading for answers, for an escape from this impending doom. But Walter merely stood there, an inscrutable expression on his face.

"You're mistaken, Detective," Walter interjected calmly, his voice dripping with self-assurance. "Solace is innocent. You won't find what you're looking for here."

Callahan scoffed, his eyes flickering with a mix of skepticism and determination. "We'll see about that. The evidence speaks for itself."

As the detective moved forward to apprehend Solace, a spark of defiance ignited within him. He couldn't let himself be taken down without a fight, without seeking the truth that eluded him for far too long.

In a sudden burst of desperation, Solace lunged forward, knocking Callahan off balance. The two men grappled with each other, their bodies colliding with the force of their struggle. Solace's heart pounded in his chest as the room filled with the sound of their labored breaths and the scuffling of their feet against the worn-out carpet.

With a surge of strength fueled by fear and determination, Solace managed to break free from Callahan's grip, staggering backward. He cast a quick glance at Walter, his eyes silently pleading for assistance. But Walter remained unmoving, his face betraying no hint of support or intervention.

Solace's mind raced, trying to piece together the fragments of the puzzle. He had trusted Walter blindly, but now he wondered if he had been nothing more than a pawn in a grander scheme. The pieces were slowly falling into place, revealing a darker truth that had remained hidden from him all along.

"Solace, don't be a fool," Walter finally spoke, his voice dripping with cold indifference. "You can't escape this. Surrender now, and I may spare your life."

A surge of anger coursed through Solace's veins, fueling his defiance. "Spare my life?" he spat, his voice laced with bitterness. "You think I would sacrifice everything, kill innocent people for you, and then be disposable once the heat is on?"

The room fell into a heavy silence as the words hung in the air. Solace's eyes bore into Walter's, a mix of betrayal and determination burning within them. He knew he had to break free from the chains of loyalty that had bound him so tightly.

.

Callahan, recovering from the scuffle, slowly regained his composure. "Solace, time is running out," he warned, his voice laced with urgency. "Cooperate with us, and we can protect you."

Solace glanced at the detective, his senses on high alert. The offer was tempting, a chance to finally sever ties with the organization and seek redemption for his actions. But he also knew that the truth, the answers he sought, lay within the web of secrets that entangled Walter Tyndale.

"No deals, Callahan," Solace replied, his voice steady. "I'll cooperate, but only if you help me expose the true extent of Walter's crimes."

A flicker of surprise passed through Callahan's eyes, followed by a glint of satisfaction. "You're making a dangerous choice, Solace," he warned. "But if you're willing to risk it all, we'll do everything we can to bring Tyndale down."

The room was filled with a renewed sense of purpose, a shared understanding between Solace and the detective. They both knew the path ahead would be treacherous, with danger lurking around every corner. But together, they held the key to unraveling the mysteries that had plagued them both.

As Solace prepared to step into a world where loyalty had become a twisted illusion, he couldn't shake the feeling that the truth he sought would be far darker and more sinister than he could have ever imagined. The scent of betrayal hung in the air, a lingering reminder of the price he had paid for misplaced trust.

With a resolute nod, Solace met Callahan's gaze, his voice filled with steely determination. "Let's bring Walter Tyndale to justice, no matter the cost."

Walter was nowhere to be found. He was long gone.

\*\*\*

As they ventured into the heart of darkness, the shadows grew longer, the sound of their footsteps echoing through the empty corridors. The air was heavy with anticipation, each step bringing them closer to the heart of the organization's labyrinthine secrets.

Solace's senses were heightened, acutely aware of every creaking floorboard and the faint scent of dampness that permeated the air. The walls seemed to whisper their secrets, their voices swirling with trepidation and hidden truths.

Callahan led the way, his eyes darting from door to door, searching for any sign of activity or potential danger. Solace followed closely behind, his muscles tensed, ready to react at a moment's notice. The weight of responsibility pressed upon him, knowing that his choices could determine not only his own fate but the fate of countless others ensnared in Walter Tyndale's web.

They reached a door at the end of the hallway, its faded paint and worn handle indicating years of neglect. Callahan turned the handle, and it groaned in protest, as if warning them of the perils that lay beyond.

The room they entered was dimly lit, the weak glow of a single overhead bulb casting eerie shadows against the walls. Solace's eyes scanned the surroundings, taking in the sight of stacked files, old photographs, and meticulously organized documents. It was a secret archive, a repository of the organization's darkest secrets.

As Solace approached a desk cluttered with papers, his fingers brushed against the cold, smooth surface. He picked up a photograph, his eyes widening in recognition. It was a picture of Walter Tyndale, but the man in the photo bore a striking resemblance to someone Solace had once known—a long-lost relative whose fate had always remained a mystery.

A surge of realization coursed through Solace's veins, connecting the dots that had eluded him for so long. The truth unraveled like an intricately woven tapestry, revealing the depth of Walter Tyndale's deception. He was not just a criminal mastermind; he was a puppeteer, manipulating lives and orchestrating tragedies for his own insidious purposes.

"Solace, what is it?" Callahan's voice broke through his thoughts, concern etched on his face.

Solace looked up, his gaze meeting Callahan's determined eyes. "Walter Tyndale isn't just a criminal, Detective," he spoke, his voice trembling with a mix of anger and disbelief. "He's my family. And he's been using me, using all of us, as pawns in his twisted game."

Callahan's jaw tightened, his fists clenched at his sides.

"Your family?" Callahan asked.

"Foster," Solace replied, looking away, his eyes on the lookout for danger.

"We have to expose him, Solace," he said, his voice filled with resolve. "We have to bring him down, no matter the cost."

Solace nodded, the weight of his newfound knowledge heavy on his shoulders. "I won't let him destroy any more lives," he vowed, his voice laced with determination. "Perhaps, it's about time to let all eyes into dark secrets."

As they prepared to leave the room, their mission clear and their resolve unwavering, Solace couldn't shake the feeling that the darkness they were about to confront was far more sinister than anything they had encountered before. The scent of danger hung in the air, mingling with the faint odor of decay, a harbinger of the trials that awaited them.

And so, with their footsteps echoing through the empty corridors, Solace and Callahan ventured forth, their resolve unyielding, their sights set on bringing down the malevolent puppeteer, Walter Tyndale. But unbeknownst to them, the tendrils of danger had already begun to tighten around their quest for truth.

As Solace and Callahan traversed the treacherous path, their senses remained on high alert. The acrid stench of burning documents assaulted their nostrils, a chilling reminder that their pursuit had not gone unnoticed. Someone within the organization knew of their intentions and was determined to eradicate any trace of evidence that could expose Walter Tyndale's true nature.

The flickering fluorescent lights cast eerie shadows, heightening the atmosphere of tension and imminent peril. Each step echoed through the desolate corridors, a constant reminder of the risks they were willing to take to unearth the truth. It was a race against time, as darkness threatened to swallow them whole.

Their journey led them deeper into the labyrinthine maze of the organization's hideout. As they turned a corner, a sudden noise shattered the silence. The screeching of metal against metal reverberated through the air, sending a shiver down their spines.

Solace and Callahan froze, their eyes narrowing as they exchanged a knowing glance. There was someone else in the shadows, a formidable force lurking in the darkness, ready to defend the secrets they sought to expose.

A figure emerged, stepping into the dim glow of a flickering light. Clad in a tailored suit, his face concealed by the shadows, he exuded an aura of ruthless authority. It was Marcus, Walter Tyndale's right-hand man, the enforcer known for his brutality and unwavering loyalty.

"Well, well, well, look what we have here," Marcus sneered, his voice dripping with venom. "Solace, I always knew you'd turn out to be a liability. But I never expected you to bring the law down on us."

Solace's heart pounded in his chest, the weight of their predicament pressing upon him. He had underestimated the reach of the organization, the lengths to which they would go to protect their leader. But he refused to back down, even in the face of imminent danger.

"Marcus, you don't have to do this," Solace said, his voice steady despite the adrenaline coursing through his veins. "We both know the truth about Walter. It's time to end this cycle of violence."

Marcus's eyes narrowed, a twisted smile playing on his lips. "You think you can save your soul, Solace? It's far too late for redemption," he spat. "Walter Tyndale is our master, our salvation. You're just a pawn who has outlived his usefulness."

In a swift motion, Marcus drew a hidden weapon from his coat, the glint of steel reflecting the wavering light. Solace and Callahan braced themselves for the imminent clash, their senses heightened, prepared to fight for their lives and the truth they sought.

But before the confrontation could escalate further, a deafening gunshot echoed through the corridor. Solace and Callahan watched in shock as Marcus stumbled backward, his grip on the weapon faltering. Blood stained his shirt, a testament to the arrival of an unexpected savior.

In the midst of the chaos, a figure emerged from the shadows, clad in a long coat and armed with a smoking gun. It was Evelyn, a skilled and enigmatic ally who had been silently watching from the sidelines, waiting for the opportune moment to reveal herself.

"Solace, we don't have much time," Evelyn warned, her voice urgent as she ignores detective Callahan. "More of them are coming. We need to move, now."

Solace's mind reeled with a mix of relief and astonishment. She could recall her vividly. She was one of the initiates on the night he first confronted Walter. He couldn't help but wonder how fast she grew up the ranks.

*She's damn gutful!*

He hadn't anticipated the presence of Evelyn, but he realized that their paths had converged for a reason. With their lives hanging in the balance, they had to trust in this enigmatic ally and continue their fight against the darkness that threatened to consume them.

As they fled through the labyrinth of secrets, Solace couldn't help but wonder how deep the rabbit hole truly went. What other revelations awaited them, and how much more would they have to sacrifice to expose the true face of Walter Tyndale?

Solace suddenly grew full trust in his two allies. Although he remained nervous about the fact that Callahan is a cop, he was cool with Evelyn. At least, he knew they both belong to the same place and are fighting the same enemy. But, after Callahan's first move. He knew he was wrong.

With a hard Krav maga move, Callahan rifled a blow into Solace's neck that he melted to the floor like heated butter. While he struggled to stagger upward, Evelyn's hard kick found his forehead and he kowtowed to the ground in a loud stud. The kick knocked out the air in him.

Smilingly, Evelyn crouched before the weak Solace and mumbled.

"Trust is a game played by the weak, Solace."

## CHAPTER 9

### Serial Killer

T HE STIFLING HEAT OF THE SUMMER night weighed heavily upon Detective Shepherd as he arrived at the scene of the latest murder. The big garage of the Sumter County Police Department's station was now tainted with the scent of death, mingling with the acrid smell of gasoline and motor oil. Flashing red and blue lights illuminated the area, casting an eerie glow over the crime scene.

Dennis Curtis, the friendly cleaner, lay sprawled on the concrete floor, his lifeless eyes staring into nothingness. The detective's gaze focused on the grotesque tableau before him. Curtis had been brutally murdered, his throat mercilessly slit, just like the previous victims. The killer's signature was unmistakable, a macabre reminder of the darkness that plagued the city.

Shepherd knelt down beside the victim, his gloved hand carefully examining the body. The texture of dried blood clung to his fingertips, as if the very essence of Curtis' life had seeped into his skin. But there was something else. A strange, foreign object nestled between the victim's fingers. Shepherd's heart quickened as he gently pried it loose, revealing a piece of torn fabric.

Examining the material, he noticed a familiar logo—a crimson eagle—stitched onto the fabric. It was the emblem of a notorious motorcycle gang known as the Crimson Vipers. It was distinctively different from the other symbol he was tracking. That was the only new thing about the murder. Every other had already become the murderer's signature to Detective Shepherd.

The detective's mind raced with possibilities. Could this be a clue to the killer's identity? Or was it a deliberate misdirection?

As Shepherd stood up, his gaze fell upon Chief Siren Beth, a stern and commanding figure, striding towards him. The chief's sharp eyes pierced through the darkness, mirroring the weight of the case that now rested upon their shoulders.

He's the Chief of the Sumter County Police Department. After the third mother in the serial, he saw a need to hit the crime scene himself. It was becoming a general concern —one never to be ignored or utterly entrusted in the care of a lone homicide detective.

"Chief," Shepherd greeted, his voice filled with urgency. "We have a clear fingerprint this time. It seems we're getting closer."

The chief's jaw tightened as he surveyed the crime scene. "Good. I want every resource available in this case, Shepherd. We can't afford any missteps. With three murders already, this case has drawn more attention than we anticipated. If we don't solve it soon, the higher-ups will take over, and our chances of catching this monster will diminish."

Shepherd nodded solemnly. "I understand, Chief. I'll pull every string I can to ensure we find the killer before they slip through our fingers."

The Chief must have wanted to look Detective Shepherd in the eyes and tell him *"I've heard a thousand times"* but he just patted him on the shoulder and looked away.

As the detective turned to leave, Siren called out, "Shepherd, be careful. We're dealing with a cunning and calculated murderer. Stay one step ahead."

Shepherd's eyes met the chief's determination etched into his features. "I won't let this case consume me, Chief. We'll catch this killer, no matter the cost."

"We've lost Hine, we can't lose you. Don't forget that!"

Shepherd tirelessly pursue every lead, scrutinizing every detail, desperate to unravel the web of darkness that ensnared Sumter County. The scent of desperation permeated the air, mingling with the stench of cigarette smoke that clung to Shepherd's clothes.

The detective found himself drawn deeper into the underbelly of the city, infiltrating seedy bars and shadowy corners where whispers of the Crimson Vipers echoed. Each encounter brought him closer to the truth, a puzzle piece waiting to be placed. He could feel the weight of the case pressing upon him, his own senses heightened as if attuned to the killer's presence.

That very evening, as the moon cast a pale glow over the desolate streets, Shepherd found himself standing in front of a worn-out building. The flickering neon sign above read "Red Hound Saloon." It was rumored to be a haven for the Crimson Vipers, a place where secrets were traded in hushed tones and alliances were forged in darkness. Shepherd took a deep breath, steeling himself for what lay ahead. He pushed open the heavy wooden doors and stepped into a realm of smoke-filled air and dimly lit corners.

This time. It wasn't a dream. He led himself there.

The room was a sensory overload. The acrid tang of whiskey mixed with the pungent scent of sweat, while the flickering lights cast distorted shadows on the worn faces of patrons. The detective's eyes scanned the room, searching for any familiar faces or potential leads. It was then that he spotted a man, his black hair slicked back, sitting alone at the end of the bar.

Shepherd approached cautiously, the weight of his purpose in every step. He took a seat beside the man, and without a word, signaled the bartender for a drink. The detective's gaze remained fixed on the suspect, his senses sharp, ready to detect the slightest hint of deception.

"Looking for something, detective?" the man said, his voice laced with a sinister edge. "Or perhaps someone?"

Shepherd turned to face him, his eyes piercing through the smoke-filled haze.

"What makes you think every man with a clean cut and cool black jacket is a cop?" Detective Shepherd said.

The man chuckled. "What makes you think we don't know that cops rarely admit their identity?" the man responded.

Detective Shepherd ignored him as he struggled to lift his cigarette. He puffed a drag and turned to the man.

"What do you know?"

Again, the man chuckled but louder this time. His hysterical laugh hijacked the attention of the newby men for a few seconds before Detective Shepherd began talking again.

"Tell me what you think I should know," Detective Shepherd said again.

Pissed off. "What the fuck are you talking about? What makes you think I know what you don't know? Do I look like some innocent-looking but dirty cop?"

Detective Shepherd smiled as he retrieved his glass of vodka from the smiling waitress. Using his right to sip from his glass he used his left to push a wad of cash in front of the man.

"Tell me what you think I don't know," he said. He nodded to the cash and then the exit door. "You can walk through the door with it if you play nice."

The man looked across his shoulder as if trying to see if they were being watched.

"What makes you think I don't know this to be some big joke?"

Detective Shepherd smiled. "This could buy a dozen bottles of beer, you know!"

The man heaved and then made to grab the money but he wasn't smart enough. Detective Shepherd stopped it.

"Slow down. Stick to the rules!"

"What do you want?" the man finally asked, showing readiness to cooperate.

"I'm looking for answers, and I believe you might have them."

A sinister smile curved the man's lips. "Do I? What makes you think I'd be willing to share? You think this money is gonna move me?"

Detective Shepherd puffed another long drag. "This has nothing to do with the money. But, it can all be yours if you don't get too harsh on me," he smirked.

"What then is this about? Why do you think I can share anything with you?"

"Because I know you're connected to the Crimson Vipers," Shepherd replied, his voice steady. "And I know you had contact with the victims."

The man's eyes narrowed, a glint of defiance flickering within them. "You don't know anything, detective. You're merely a pawn in a much bigger game."

Shepherd leaned in closer, his tone low and dangerous. "Tell me what you know, and maybe I'll consider playing along."

The man chuckled, the sound carrying a chilling undertone. "You're in over your head, detective. This county hides many secrets, and those who seek them often pay the price."

Before Shepherd could respond, a sudden commotion erupted from the entrance of the saloon. The heavy doors swung open with a force, revealing a group of menacing figures clad in leather jackets adorned with the emblem of the Crimson Vipers. The air grew thick with tension as they made their way inside, their gazes fixated on Shepherd and the man at the bar.

The lead biker stepped forward, his voice dripping with menace. "Seems like you've been asking too many questions, detective."

Shepherd's hand instinctively reached for his holster, ready for the storm that was about to unleash. But the man beside him placed a restraining hand on his arm, his voice calm yet laced with warning.

"Choose your battles wisely, detective," he said, his eyes locked with Shepherd's. "Some secrets are better left buried."

In that moment, Shepherd realized he stood at a precipice, torn between his thirst for justice and the dangerous depths that lurked within the city. The fate of the investigation, the lives lost, and his own survival hung in the balance.

The deafening silence that followed hung heavy in the air, each heartbeat echoing like a distant drum. Detective Shepherd's gaze flickered between the man beside him and the imposing figures of the Crimson Viper's closing in. The weight of his duty tugged at him, urging him to confront the darkness head-on.

With steely resolve, Shepherd pushed back his chair, rising to his feet. His hand remained at his side, fingers tracing the grip of his weapon, ready to defend himself if needed. He locked eyes with the lead biker, his voice firm and unwavering.

"I won't back down," Shepherd declared, his words carrying the weight of his conviction. "Not until I uncover the truth and bring justice to those who have fallen."

A murmur of anticipation rippled through the crowd as the tension reached its zenith. The biker's lip curled into a sneer, a dangerous glimmer flickering in his eyes. "So be it, detective. You've chosen your path."

As if on cue, chaos erupted. The Crimson Vipers lunged forward, their movements swift and predatory. Fists flew and the screech of breaking glass mingled with the cries of pain. Shepherd skillfully dodged a swing aimed at his jaw, retaliating with a calculated strike that sent his attacker sprawling to the floor.

The detective fought with a desperate determination, his senses heightened in the heat of the battle. The sharp scent of sweat and the metallic tang of blood mingled in the air as blows landed and bodies collided. It was a dance of survival, a struggle against the encroaching darkness.

Amidst the fray, Shepherd caught a glimpse of the man he had confronted earlier, the one who held the answers. Their eyes locked for a fleeting moment, and an unspoken understanding passed between them. With a swift nod, the man disappeared into the chaos, leaving Shepherd to face his foes alone.

The fight raged on, each passing second feeling like an eternity. Shepherd's vision narrowed, focusing solely on his adversaries. He ducked, weaved, and countered, using every ounce of his training to stay one step ahead. But the odds were stacked against him, the bikers relentless in their pursuit.

As the tide of battle turned, Shepherd found himself backed against a wall, surrounded by a sea of hostility. Adrenaline coursed through his veins, his heart pounding in his chest. Aching muscles and the sting of bruises served as reminders of the price he would pay for standing against the darkness.

Just as it seemed the detective would be overwhelmed, a resounding crash shattered the cacophony. The doors of the saloon swung open once again, revealing a squad of uniformed officers, their badges glinting under the neon lights. The room fell into a stunned silence as the police reinforcements flooded the scene, subduing the remaining members of the Crimson Vipers with swift efficiency. The battle was over, and the darkness had been momentarily quelled.

Detective Shepherd leaned against the wall, his breath ragged and labored. He looked around, his eyes scanning the room for any sign of the enigmatic man who had vanished amidst the chaos. But he was nowhere to be found. The truth-seeker had slipped away, leaving Shepherd with more questions than answers.

Chief Siren, his expression a mix of relief and concern, approached the detective through the dissipating haze of the aftermath. "Shepherd, what in the hell happened here?"

Shepherd straightened, his gaze meeting Siren's with a mix of exhaustion and determination. "I followed a lead, Chief. It led me to the Crimson Vipers, and things escalated from there."

"And?" Chief asked in a tone Detective Shepherd rarely heard him use.

"We had a momentary clash."

He's in trouble.

Siren's eyes narrowed, his voice filled with a mixture of frustration and admiration.

"You've stirred up a hornet's nest, Shepherd. This case is spiraling out of control. We've managed to quell this skirmish, but if we don't make headway soon, the higher-ups will take over, and our chances of catching the mastermind behind all this will dwindle."

"I only need answers, Chief!"

"At the wrong place, Shepherd."

"I don't think so. I saw him. We made progress. But…"

Chief Siren turned to him

"But what?"

"They interrogated and let him escape. He knows what they don't."

"That was unethical, Shepherd!"

His brows furrowed, Shepherd keeled aside. "Chief I…I…I apologize for…"

"Not now. This is far more dangerous than you think it is. We are a team…we don't make lone moves. Hine must have been killed in a similar clash or its aftermath. Who knows? Do we plan to let this slide by committing avoidable blunders?"

Shepherd's resolve hardened, a flicker of defiance igniting within him. "I won't let that happen, Chief. I won't let this county fall into the hands of darkness. I'll find him. No matter the cost."

Siren regarded Shepherd for a moment, his gaze intense yet filled with a begrudging respect. "You've always been a stubborn one, Shepherd. I can't say I approve of your methods, but damn it, I believe in your ability to get the job done. But tread carefully. This case has taken a turn for the worse, and the stakes have never been higher."

With a nod, Shepherd watched as Chief Siren rallied his officers, organizing the arrest of the subdued bikers.

The room gradually emptied, leaving behind the remnants of the battle that had unfolded within its walls. Shepherd knew that time was of the essence, that every passing moment brought him closer to the edge of the abyss.

As he stepped out into the cool night air, a gust of wind brushed against his face, carrying with it the scent of uncertainty. The shadows danced around him, whispering their secrets and taunting him to delve deeper into the unknown. Shepherd knew that he was on the precipice of a treacherous journey, one that would test his resolve and push him to his limits.

With the echoes of the recent clash still ringing in his ears, Detective Shepherd set his sights on the next lead, determined to follow the trail of darkness wherever it may lead.

## CHAPTER 10

### Who Are They?

I T'S OFFICIALLY A KILLING SPREE. There are no two explanations for it.

The rain-soaked streets of the city reflected the flickering neon lights, casting an eerie glow on the scene. Detective Shepherd stood under the awning of the Olive Boulevard train station, as he watched the forensics team meticulously comb through the evidence.

The murder of renowned socialite Victoria Beaumont had sent shockwaves through the county and now they had a suspect in their sights. Perhaps, that very murder would be the last stroke that'd break the camel's back.

Samuel Miller, the gardener at the train station, had suddenly become the center of attention. All the evidence they had gathered pointed to him, but Detective Shepherd knew better than to jump to conclusions. He had seen too many cases where things were not as they seemed.

As the rain continued to patter against the pavement, Detective Shepherd made his way towards the station's gardener shed. The smell of damp earth mixed with the tang of freshly cut grass hung in the air. He pushed open the creaking door, revealing Samuel Miller hunched over a workbench, tending to a row of potted plants.

"Mr. Miller," Detective Shepherd announced his arrival, his voice low and authoritative. "Detective Shepherd, homicide division. I need to ask you a few questions."

Miller turned around, surprise etched on his weathered face. He wiped his hands on his worn-out denim overalls and studied the detective with cautious eyes. "Detective, what's this all about? I didn't have anything to do with that lady's murder."

Detective Shepherd leaned against the doorframe, his gaze fixed on Miller. "All the evidence we've gathered points to you, Mr. Miller. We found your fingerprints on areas around the scene, and witnesses saw you leaving the axis of the scene."

Miller's eyes widened in disbelief. "But that's impossible! I never even knew the lady. I've been working here all day."

"You never knew Victoria Beaumont?" he asked.

Miller stammered. "Not particularly. I see her on the news but can't really say I can't spot her in a crowd."

"Is that right?" Detective Shepherd countered, her tone sharp. "Can anyone vouch for your whereabouts during the time of the murder?"

Miller hesitated, his gaze shifting to the rain-soaked ground. "Well, I don't know. I mostly keep to myself, you see. But I might be able to help you with something else."

Detective Shepherd's interest was piqued. "What do you mean?"

Miller took a step closer, his voice barely above a whisper. "I've seen things, detective. I've seen the people who come and go from this station. I might have noticed something out of the ordinary that could help your investigation."

Detective Shepherd leaned in, his eyes narrowing. "What have you seen, Miller?"

For the next hour, Miller revealed a string of suspicious encounters he had witnessed at the train station. Shadows lurking in the darkness, whispered conversations, and furtive glances. Detective Shepherd listened intently, his mind racing to connect the dots. Each word from Miller painted a vivid picture of a hidden underworld operating beneath the bustling city streets.

The scent of musty soil and the cool touch of rain-soaked air wrapped around Detective Shepherd as he absorbed the gardener's words. The sense of sight had revealed the evidence, but it was the senses of smell and touch that connected her to the truth hidden within the station's secrets.

As the interview drew to a close, Detective Shepherd's phone buzzed in her pocket. She retrieved it, glancing at the screen—a message from her partner, Detective Brown. The message read:

*"Found something big. Meet me at the abandoned warehouse on Elm Street. Hurry."*

Detective Shepherd's heart quickened. The pieces of the puzzle were finally falling into place, and he knew time was of the essence. He turned to Miller with a sense of urgency in her eyes.

"Mr. Miller," Detective Shepherd said, her voice firm. "Thank you for your cooperation. Your information might prove invaluable to this case. Stay here and let the officers know if anything else comes to mind. I need to follow up on a lead."

Miller nodded, his eyes filled with a mixture of relief and curiosity. "Detective, I hope you find the truth. There's something rotten in this place, and it needs to be exposed."

Detective Shepherd gave him a reassuring nod before rushing out of the shed and into the pouring rain. He flagged a cab and directed the driver to the abandoned warehouse on Elm Street, where Detective Brown awaited her.

The cab sped through the slick streets, raindrops cascading down the windows like tears on a somber night. Detective Shepherd's mind raced, his senses heightened. The scent of wet asphalt filled the car, mixing with the sharp tang of anticipation. He tapped her fingers anxiously against her thigh and played shanty beats with his legs, feeling the vibrations of anticipation reverberating through her body.

Finally, the cab screeched to a halt in front of the darkened warehouse. Detective Shepherd paid the driver and stepped out into the night, pulling her coat tighter around her frame. The warehouse loomed before her, its dilapidated exterior a haunting reminder of forgotten secrets.

She entered the abandoned building cautiously, her footsteps echoing through the empty space. Detective Brown emerged from the shadows, his face etched with determination.

"Come on. You might want to see what I've found," Detective Brown said, his voice hushed yet urgent. "This place is some saucy den of de. Stumbled upon something big."

Detective Shepherd's pulse quickened. Although his hope had gotten used to staying low, he knew they were on the verge of unraveling the web of lies surrounding Victoria Beaumont's murder or something closer. He gestured for Detective Brown to lead the way, their steps cautious as they ventured deeper into the warehouse's depths.

The air grew heavy, the scent of mildew mingling with the acrid tang of fear. The dim lighting cast eerie shadows that danced on the cracked walls. Detective Shepherd's fingers brushed against dusty surfaces, feeling the gritty texture of neglect. Each step forward intensified the suspense, heightening his senses and sharpening her focus.

As they explored further, they stumbled upon a hidden room concealed behind a false wall. Detective Brown's flashlight illuminated a scene that sent shivers down their spines. Documents, photographs, and surveillance equipment adorned the walls—a labyrinth of information perhaps, connecting the powerful and the corrupt.

Detective Shepherd's eyes widened as he spotted a familiar face among the photographs. It was Victoria Beaumont, captured in compromising positions with influential figures. The pieces of the puzzle were falling into place, revealing a clandestine world fueled by power, greed, and unspeakable secrets.

Before they could process the magnitude of their discovery, the sound of footsteps echoed from the darkness beyond. Detective Shepherd and Detective Brown exchanged a glance, their hearts pounding in unison. They darted behind a stack of crates, concealed but vulnerable.

Through the gap between crates, they watched as a group of armed individuals entered the hidden room, their whispered conversations laced with menace. It was clear they were no ordinary criminals—they were the puppeteers pulling the strings, orchestrating a macabre dance of deception.

One of the figures turned their way, scanning the room with a calculating gaze. Detective Shepherd's breath caught in his throat as their eyes locked for a fleeting moment. He could almost taste the danger in the air, the metallic tang of impending confrontation.

With a silent nod, Detective Shepherd and Detective Brown made a silent pact. They would delve deeper into this sinister web, exposing the truth and bringing justice to the innocent. The stakes had never been higher, and they knew they had to tread carefully, like a pair of panthers stalking their prey.

As the armed figures moved away, Detective Shepherd and Detective Brown emerged from their hiding place, their minds racing with questions and their bodies pulsing with adrenaline. They needed to unravel the intricate threads that connected the corrupt elite to Victoria Beaumont's murder and bring them to justice.

"We can't let them get away with this," Detective Brown whispered, his voice filled with determination. "We need to dig deeper, find concrete evidence that will expose their web of deceit."

Detective Shepherd nodded in agreement, his eyes gleaming with unwavering resolve. "No less unfollowed. No stone unturned. We owe it to Detective Hine and all the innocent lives affected by this web of darkness."

They ventured further into the hidden room, meticulously examining the documents and photographs that adorned the walls. Each piece of evidence uncovered revealed a twisted tale of power, manipulation, and unspeakable acts. It was as if the room held the keys to unlocking the truth, but they had to decipher the puzzle before them.

As they sifted through the papers, Detective Shepherd's fingers brushed against a photograph that made his blood sizzle. It depicted a secret meeting, high-ranking officials and influential figures gathered in a luxurious mansion, their faces twisted by sinister intentions. Among them was a face she recognized—Samuel Miller, the gardener from the train station.

"This goes deeper than we thought," Detective Brown murmured, her voice tinged with a mixture of shock and determination. "Miller wasn't just a witness; he's part of their game. But what role does he play?"

Detective Shepherd's eyes narrowed, his gaze piercing through the shadows. "Signal the patrols, Brown. I need him in the interrogation room."

As they prepared to leave the warehouse, a creaking sound echoed through the room, followed by the unmistakable click of a gun. They turned to face the source of the noise, their hearts pounding in their chests.

Standing before them, gun in hand, was Samuel Miller. His weathered face twisted into a sinister smile as he spoke with a chilling calmness.

"Detective Shepherd, Detective Brown, how wonderful of you to join us. It seems you've stumbled upon something you shouldn't have," Miller said, his voice dripping with malice. "You're a thorn in their side, just like Victoria was. But unlike her, you won't make it out alive."

Detective Shepherd and Detective Brown exchanged a glance, their eyes silently communicating a shared determination and readiness to fight. They had walked into a trap, but they wouldn't go down without a fight.

The scent of danger hung heavy in the air as the stand-off intensified. With their senses heightened, Detective Shepherd and Detective Brown prepared to face the darkness head-on, knowing that their fight for justice had just taken an even more treacherous turn.

\*\*\*

Detective Shepherd's mind raced, searching for a way out of the perilous situation. The taste of danger lingered on his tongue as he assessed their surroundings. The warehouse seemed like a labyrinth of shadows, concealing both threats and potential escape routes.

"Miller, you're making a grave mistake," Detective Brown's voice rang out, his tone filled with steely resolve. "We won't rest until we expose the truth and bring the guilty to justice."

Miller's eyes narrowed, his grip on the gun tightening. "Justice? You think justice can prevail in a world governed by power and corruption? You're naïve, Detective."

Detective Shepherd carefully edged toward a stack of crates, his eyes never leaving Miller's menacing figure. He knew that one wrong move could seal their fate. The sound of rain pounding against the roof intensified, creating a backdrop of chaotic urgency.

In a sudden burst of movement, Miller fired a shot, the deafening sound reverberating through the warehouse. Detective Brown instinctively dove for cover, his heart pounding against his chest like it'd rip it open. The bullet grazed his arm, leaving a searing trail of pain.

Detective Shepherd retaliated, returning fire with precise aim. Bullets ricocheted off the walls, shattering the silence with their deadly symphony. The air was thick with the acrid smell of gunpowder, mixing with the scent of dampness that permeated the warehouse.

Amidst the chaos, Detective Brown's senses heightened. The touch of his injured arm throbbed, reminding him of the danger they faced. He gritted her teeth, pushing through the pain, and focused on his surroundings.

His eyes caught a glimmer of light emanating from a partially open door at the far end of the warehouse. It was a sliver of hope, an opportunity for escape. He gestured urgently to Detective Brown, directing her attention to the exit.

With a shared understanding, they maneuvered through the labyrinthine paths, dodging bullets and debris. The scent of fear mingled with determination as they closed in on their only chance for survival.

As they reached the door, Detective Brown's hand brushed against the rough texture of a rusty doorknob. The sensation of touch grounded him in the present moment, fueling his resolve to overcome the darkness that threatened to consume them.

They burst out into the rain-soaked night, their footsteps blending with the symphony of thunder and rain. They didn't look back, knowing that their pursuers were hot on their trail. The senses of sight, smell, touch, and sound heightened their awareness of the danger that lurked behind them.

They raced through the desolate streets, their senses in overdrive, searching for any sign of refuge. The flickering neon lights reflected off rain-soaked pavements, casting an otherworldly glow. Each alleyway and shadow held the potential for ambush, making every step a calculated risk.

Miller made ahead. They didn't want him to live. It was avoidable but Detective Shepherd wouldn't let it slide. He had to be chased, arrested or gunned down.

***

As the sun dipped below the horizon, casting an orange glow over Sumter County, Detective Shepherd received an anonymous message. It contained a cryptic clue that would lead them closer to the heart of the conspiracy. It was a rendezvous point—an abandoned factory on the outskirts of town.

After many chases, the cop held shreds of doubts if it'd turn out successful but he'd never know if he didn't try. Meanwhile, Miller was on the run and had to be caught.

Detective Brown's eyes sparked with anticipation as they prepared to embark on another dangerous journey. The scent of determination filled the air as they set out, each step brimming with a mix of anticipation and apprehension.

The abandoned factory loomed before them, its decaying walls a testament to the secrets it held. They stepped cautiously through broken glass and discarded remnants of forgotten industry. The smell of rust and decay mixed with the scent of something more sinister—a lingering odor of fear and desperation.

As they ventured deeper into the factory, their senses were assaulted by the sights and sounds of a clandestine gathering. Shadowy figures huddled together, their whispers echoing in the cavernous space. Detective Shepherd and Detective Brown remained hidden, observing from the shadows, their senses attuned to every detail.

The sense of sight revealed familiar faces among the gathering—the very figures they had been pursuing. It was a web of deception, extending far beyond what they had imagined. But there was one person, an enigmatic figure, who stood at the center of it all. It was a man whose influence reached far and whose touch tainted everything it came into contact with.

Detective Shepherd's heart raced as she watched the man, her senses on high alert. He could almost taste the power emanating from him, the unmistakable scent of corruption. This man held the key to unraveling the conspiracy, the one who could expose the hidden truths they sought.

But before they could make their move, an unexpected noise reverberated through the factory. A sharp, metallic click followed by a low, menacing chuckle. Detective Shepherd's senses went into overdrive as he realized they had walked into yet another trap.

The lights flickered to life, casting an unforgiving glare on the scene. Surrounding them were armed men, their guns pointed with deadly precision. It was a betrayal they hadn't seen coming, a betrayal that had deceived their heightened senses.

From the corner of his eye, Detective Shepherd caught a glimpse of the enigmatic figure stepping forward, a sadistic smile curling his lips. " Detective Shepherd," he sneered. "I must commend you on your persistence. I mean, one wouldn't have to wonder why you were a first choice at the Police academy."

Detective Shepherd exchanged a knowing glance with Detective Brown. Their senses were still heightened, their minds sharp despite the impending danger. They refused to let the darkness consume them. They had come too far to turn back now.

With a steely resolve, Detective Shepherd stepped forward, his voice steady and unwavering. "You may have us trapped for now, but the truth will always find its way to the surface. We will expose your web of deceit, no matter the cost."

The enigmatic figure's laughter echoed through the factory, mocking their determination. "Oh, Detective Shepherd, you underestimate the power that lies within these walls," he retorted, his voice dripping with arrogance. "You may have unraveled some threads, but the true extent of this conspiracy is far beyond your grasp. Prepare to meet your end."

The armed men closed in, their footsteps resounding in the vast space. Detective Shepherd's mind raced, seeking a way to turn the tide in their favor. Their lives depended on their next move.

In a sudden burst of action, Detective Brown seized a nearby metal pipe, swinging it with precision and striking one of the armed men. The clanging sound reverberated through the factory, momentarily disorienting their assailants. It was a split-second opportunity that Detective Shepherd didn't waste.

He lunged forward, his senses on high alert. The smell of sweat and adrenaline filled the air as he swiftly disarmed another assailant, snatching his gun. Shots rang out, punctuating the chaos, as Detective Shepherd returned fire, creating a path of temporary reprieve.

"Fall back!" Detective Shepherd commanded, his voice projecting with authority. He and Detective Brown retreated further into the depths of the factory, their senses attuned to the pursuit of survival.

As they weaved through the labyrinthine corridors, their footsteps echoed with urgency. Detective Shepherd's mind raced, contemplating their next move. They needed a way out, a chance to regroup and continue their fight against the corruption creeping towards them.

In a moment of desperation, Detective Shepherd's senses led him to a door at the far end of a dimly lit hallway. He could feel a draft of fresh air seeping through the cracks, a glimmer of freedom amidst the darkness.

With a burst of strength, he kicked the door open, revealing an abandoned rooftop overlooking the cityscape. The rain poured down, drenching them to the bone, but they pushed forward, their determination unfaltering.

As they sprinted across the rain-soaked rooftop, Detective Shepherd's senses heightened. He could smell the wet asphalt and feel the texture of the gritty rooftop beneath her fingertips. The taste of freedom lingered in the air, a tantalizing promise of escape.

But just as they reached the edge of the rooftop, ready to descend to safety, a voice pierced through the night, freezing them in their tracks.

"There's nowhere left to run."

They turned to face the enigmatic figure, his silhouette framed against the city lights. Behind him, his armed henchmen closed in, forming a formidable barrier.

"You may have evaded us for now, but there will be no escape this time," he taunted, his voice laced with triumph. "Let's draw the curtain here."

Detective Shepherd's skedaddled, his senses on overdrive. He knew that their fight had reached a critical juncture. They were cornered, with nowhere to hide and no allies to rely on.

But Detective Shepherd refused to surrender. He locked eyes with Detective Brown, a silent understanding passing between them. They had come too far to let their pursuit of justice end in defeat.

With a determined glare, Detective Shepherd spoke, his voice cutting through the tension-filled air. "We may be trapped, but the truth will always find its way. We will not rest until justice is served."

As the enigmatic figure raised his gun, ready to deliver the final blow, a sudden crash interrupted the scene. The rooftop door behind them burst open, and a group of shadowy figures emerged, armed and ready for battle.

Detective Shepherd's heart soared with renewed hope. He and Detective Brown were not alone. Allies had arrived, their arrival shattering the figure's moment of triumph.

A fierce firefight erupted on the rain-soaked rooftop, bullets whizzing through the air and piercing the silence of the night. The scent of gun smoke mingled with the earthy aroma of rain, creating an intoxicating blend that fueled their determination.

Detective Shepherd and Detective Brow fought side by side, their senses finely attuned to the chaos unfolding around them. They exchanged knowing glances, their unspoken bond strengthening their resolve. With their newfound allies, they pushed forward, inching closer to victory.

Amidst the relentless exchange of gunfire, the figure's confident façade crumbled. Fear flashed in his eyes as he realized that his grip on power was slipping away. His armed henchmen faltered, their ranks diminishing with every well-aimed shot.

The tide had turned, and justice surged forward with unstoppable force. Detective Shepherd and Detective Brown fought with unwavering determination, their senses honed to a razor's edge. They had become warriors of truth, relentlessly pursuing those who believed they were untouchable.

As the firefight raged on, the figure made a desperate move, attempting to escape the rooftop. But Detective Shepherd, her senses heightened and reflexes sharpened, intercepted his path. He tackled him to the ground, their bodies colliding with a resounding thud.

"No room for a run," Detective Shepherd hissed, his voice laced with fury and triumph. He restrained him, his fingers digging into his flesh, the sensation of touch serving as a reminder that justice had prevailed.

Detective Brown swiftly secured the remaining threats, their reign of terror finally coming to an end. The rooftop was now engulfed in a tense silence, broken only by the sound of heavy breathing and raindrops cascading from the eaves.

The figure, defeated and powerless, looked up at Detective Shepherd with a mix of defiance and resignation. "You may have won this battle, but the war... the war is far from over," he muttered, his voice filled with bitterness.

Detective Shepherd leaned closer, her voice low and cutting. "We will dismantle your network piece by piece, expose the truth, and ensure that justice prevails. I think this is ending here."

With a final glance at the defeated figure, Detective Shepherd rose to his feet, his senses still heightened, ever vigilant. The battle had taken its toll, but the pursuit of truth had triumphed. They had uncovered the darkness that lurked beneath the surface, and now it was time to bring it into the light.

Having handcuffed him, Detective Shepherd finally took off the figure's silicon mask, dashing back as his face got clearer.

It's Samuel Miller.

Detective Brown didn't respond when Miller made a silly move. He had snapped out of his cuffs and none of the cops could say how. He grabbed Detective Brown's gun from his pouch, cocked the gun and blew up his head, smearing the wall with his blood.

*Shit!*

## CHAPTER 11

### Never Say No

S    OLACE LOST IT. All of it. He lost the usual ecstasy that comes with working for Walter and his dark organization. His senses heightened by the weight of the council's demand. After being arrested by fake Detective Callahan and Evelyn, taking another task became a must for him.

The air was heavy with the scent of tension, mingling with the faint aroma of cigars that lingered from their earlier meeting. His mind raced, grappling with the gravity of the task that had been thrust upon him.

The council, a shadowy group of power brokers who operated in the underworld, had summoned Solace to discuss a new assignment. Their eyes glinted with cold determination as they delivered their edict—a reputable probation officer in Benton Ridge had become a thorn in their side. They wanted him eliminated, and they expected Solace to be the instrument of their vengeance. It was his punishment for attempting to revolt against the organization.

Solace's instinct for survival screamed at him to refuse, to sever ties with the organization that had ensnared him. But Walter, the council's enforcer, issued a chilling warning. "Cross us, Solace, and you'll face consequences far worse than you can imagine. Remember, you're in this too deep."

The pressure weighed heavily on Solace's shoulders, threatening to crush his resolve. He knew the probation officer in question—Daniel Simmons—a man dedicated to reforming the lives of those who had lost their way. Killing him would be an act of injustice, a betrayal of his own moral code.

As the council's meeting drew to a close, Solace found himself alone in the room, grappling with his decision. The sound of his own heartbeat reverberated in his ears, a reminder of the stakes involved. He knew that time was not on his side; he had only two days to carry out the task or face the wrath of Walter and the council.

The next morning, Solace set out for Benton Ridge, his senses attuned to the sights and sounds of the city. He navigated the streets, his fingers tracing the rough texture of the steering wheel, his mind consumed by conflicting emotions. The scent of rain hung in the air, a metaphorical cleansing that whispered the possibility of redemption.

Arriving in *Benton Ridge*, Solace found himself in the quiet neighborhood where Daniel Simmons resided. He observed from a distance, his gaze fixed on the modest house that held the man's aspirations for a better future. The sight of children playing in nearby yards stirred something deep within him—a flicker of humanity that threatened to jeopardize the mission.

As dusk settled over the neighborhood, Solace found himself standing outside Daniel's house, shadows enveloping his figure. He couldn't shake the image of Walter's threatening words from his mind. The pressure weighed on him like an invisible shackle, constricting his every breath.

His senses heightened as he approached the front door, his gloved hand brushing against the rough texture of the wood. He hesitated, a flood of memories flooding his mind—memories of a life he had left behind, of a time when justice was more than a mere illusion.

In a moment of defiance, Solace stepped back, his resolve hardening. He couldn't bring himself to carry out this act of darkness. It was time to sever the ties that bound him to the council, to reclaim his own moral compass. He refused to be a pawn in their game any longer.

But just as he turned to leave, a voice from the shadows froze him in his tracks. "Solace, I knew you'd struggle with this decision. How disappointing."

Walter emerged, his eyes cold and merciless. Solace's heart pounded in his chest as Walter drew closer, his imposing presence dominating the scene. "You think you can walk away? Think again, Solace. There's no escaping the council's reach."

Solace's mind raced, his senses on high alert. He had walked into yet another trap, his instincts screaming at him to find a way out. The scent of danger hung in the air, mingling with the acrid tang of fear. He had to think quickly, to find a path to freedom before Walter's wrath consumed him.

With a surge of adrenaline, Solace took a step back, his hand inching toward the concealed weapon at his side. His eyes never left Walter's, searching for any sign of weakness or distraction. He had survived this long by trusting his senses, and now they guided him toward his next move.

"I won't be your pawn any longer, Walter," Solace growled, his voice laced with determination. "There's a darkness within me, but I refuse to let it define me. I'm breaking free from this cycle of violence."

Walter's lips curled into a malevolent grin, his hand reaching for the hidden knife strapped to his leg. "You're making a grave mistake, Solace. The council doesn't take defiance lightly. You will regret this."

As Walter lunged forward, the scene erupted into a desperate struggle. Solace's senses kicked into overdrive, his body reacting with the precision of a trained warrior. He could feel the impact of Walter's blows against his flesh, the searing pain igniting his determination.

In a burst of strength, Solace managed to disarm Walter, their bodies locked in a fierce dance of survival. The taste of copper filled his mouth as a stray punch landed, but he fought through the pain, his focus unwavering. He knew that his only chance was to incapacitate Walter and escape this deadly trap.

With a swift, calculated move, Solace delivered a devastating blow that sent Walter crashing to the ground. He seized the opportunity, his senses guiding him toward the exit, toward freedom. Every fiber of his being screamed for him to run, to leave this life behind.

But just as Solace reached the threshold of escape, a gunshot shattered the air. A searing pain tore through his shoulder, his body wrenching with the impact. He stumbled, his vision swimming as he fought to stay conscious. Blood soaked through his clothes, staining the fabric a deep crimson.

Through the haze of pain, Solace's gaze locked onto the figure that had fired the shot. It wasn't Walter. It was someone else—a hired gun, sent by the council to ensure he never walked away. The scent of betrayal hung heavy in the air, mingling with the metallic tang of blood.

Solace's strength wavered, his body growing weaker by the second. The world around him blurred, sounds fading into a distant echo. He knew he had to keep moving, to find help, but his limbs felt heavy, unresponsive.

As darkness closed in on the edges of his vision, Solace whispered a promise to himself, a vow that he would not let his story end here. With his last ounce of strength, he dragged himself toward the shadows, seeking refuge from the impending threat.

The outcome remained uncertain, but Solace's spirit burned with an unyielding determination. He would fight against the council's grip, against the darkness that threatened to consume him. The taste of vengeance lingered on his lips, a reminder that his journey was far from over.

In the depths of pain and uncertainty, Solace clung to his resolve, his senses attuned to the flickering flame of hope.

A few more steps, he dashed into the heart of the night—far away from the deadly eyes of Walter and the shooter.

\*\*\*

Solace lay hidden in the shadows, his body battered and weak. The scent of his own blood filled his nostrils, mingling with the dank smell of the alleyway where he sought refuge. The pain radiated through his wounded shoulder, threatening to consume him entirely. But Solace refused to surrender. He clung to consciousness with a stubborn determination, knowing that his survival depended on it.

His eyes scanned the dimly lit alley, searching for any sign of his pursuers. The dim glow of a flickering streetlight illuminated the rain-soaked pavement, casting eerie shadows that danced like specters. Solace's senses, honed by years of survival, heightened to their utmost potential. He listened for the faintest of footsteps, the rustle of fabric, anything that might reveal his enemy's presence.

The sound of distant sirens pierced the night air, growing closer with each passing moment. Solace knew he couldn't rely on the authorities for help, not when the council's influence reached far and wide. He had to find a way to tend to his wounds, to disappear into the underbelly of the county until he could reclaim his strength.

With great effort, Solace pushed himself up, the pain throbbing through every fiber of his being. He stumbled forward, his hand brushing against the cold brick wall for support. The texture, rough and unforgiving, served as a reminder of the harsh reality he faced.

As he made his way through the labyrinthine alleys, Solace's eyes darted from shadow to shadow, his body tense and ready for any threat that might reveal itself. The county whispered its secrets, a symphony of distant car horns and muffled conversations, but Solace knew he had to remain vigilant. The council's reach extended into every corner of this metropolis, and danger lurked in even the most mundane of places.

After what felt like an eternity of navigating the treacherous urban maze, Solace stumbled upon a decrepit building that had been forgotten by time. The flickering neon sign above the entrance advertised a long-defunct bar, its once vibrant colors faded and chipped. Solace knew this was his chance—a chance to find shelter, to tend to his wounds, and to regroup.

He pushed open the creaking door, the musty smell of stale beer hitting his nostrils. The dimly lit interior was devoid of life, save for a lone figure sitting at the far end of the bar. The bartender, a grizzled old man with weathered hands, looked up from cleaning a glass, his eyes filled with a mixture of curiosity and wariness.

"What brings you here, son?" the bartender asked, his voice a gravelly rasp that echoed through the empty space.

Solace approached the bar, his movements slow and deliberate. He winced as he settled onto a stool, the pain in his shoulder intensifying. "I need help," he managed to say, his voice strained. "I'm being hunted."

The bartender's eyes narrowed, his gaze flickering with a mixture of suspicion and empathy. "You're in a bad way, son," he said, his tone tinged with caution. "But this ain't no place for someone running from trouble."

Solace clenched his jaw, his determination unyielding. "I have nowhere else to go. I can't let them win."

"Them?" the man asked, despatching speeded-up glances around.

"Yeah. Forget about them. J-just. Can you clean my wound?" Solace begged.

The bartender studied him for a moment, his weathered face etched with lines that told tales of a life lived. Finally, he nodded, a glimmer of something resembling respect in his eyes. "You're a stubborn one, I'll give you that," he said. "Come on, in."

"I've seen my fair share of trouble, and I know when someone's fighting for their life. Take a seat, son. Let's see what we can do."

Solace sank deeper into the worn-out stool, gratitude washing over him. The weight of the world seemed to momentarily lift from his weary shoulders as the bartender poured a stiff drink and slid it across the counter. The scent of aged whiskey wafted toward Solace, mingling with the dusty air of the abandoned bar.

"You're not the first one to find refuge here," the bartender spoke softly, a hint of melancholy in his voice. "Sometimes, people end up on the wrong side of the law or get caught up in something they never asked for. It's a cruel world out there, but I've learned that sometimes it takes a bit of darkness to appreciate the light."

Solace nodded, taking a sip of the whiskey. The liquid burned its way down his throat, momentarily distracting him from the searing pain in his shoulder. He welcomed the warmth spreading through his body, fortifying him for the challenges that lay ahead.

As the minutes turned into hours, the bartender tended to Solace's wounds with the care of someone who had seen their fair share of injuries. The sting of antiseptic and the gentle touch of gauze against his wound were a stark reminder of the battles he had fought and the battles yet to come.

"Son, I can't promise you an easy path," the bartender said, his eyes filled with a mixture of wisdom and caution. "But I can tell you this: there's strength in embracing the darkness. Sometimes, to defeat the monsters, you have to become one."

Solace looked at the bartender, his gaze unwavering. He understood the truth behind the words—the path he had chosen was one that required sacrifice, a dance with shadows that threatened to consume him. But he refused to let it break him. He would wield the darkness, not let it wield him.

"I won't let them win," Solace declared, his voice filled with determination. "I'll track down the council and do what has to be done. No matter the cost."

The bartender's eyes narrowed, a spark of admiration glinting within them. "The council?"

Solace winced. Perhaps, pain was making him say more than he had to. "I'm sorry. I can't tell you these things…

"No. You don't have to. It's alright. I totally understand," the cut him in, surrendering the bottle of hot balm to the old rickety table. "You're a rare breed, son. The world needs more people like you, willing to fight against the tides of evil. Just remember, the line between justice and vengeance is a thin one. Don't lose sight of who you are."

*"Don't lose sight of who you are."*

Solace nodded, his gaze hardening with a newfound resolve. He knew the path ahead would be treacherous, filled with uncertainty and peril. But he also knew that he couldn't turn back. The scent of justice hung in the air, intertwining with the lingering aroma of whiskey and the echoes of the bartender's words.

As endless thoughts permeate his head, his senses heightened once again, attuned to the sights, sounds, and scents that would guide his journey. He had a score to settle, a debt to collect from those who thought they could control him. Again, the bartender's words came alive.

*"Don't lose sight of who you are."*

# CHAPTER 12

## Windless Storm

D ETECTIVE SHEPHERD STOOD outside the crumbling warehouse, his senses on high alert. The pungent odor of gunpowder and stale sweat hung heavy in the air, mingling with the acrid stench of desperation. Blood dripped from a fresh wound on his forehead, its metallic tang staining the collar of his shirt. He wiped away the crimson trail, his touch cautious and deliberate.

Around him, chaos reigned. The sound of gunfire echoed through the dilapidated building, the deafening cracks tearing through the silence of the night. Shepherd's team fought valiantly, their bullets whizzing through the smoke-filled air, seeking their mark. But the gangsters were entrenched, their numbers and firepower overwhelming.

They had walked into a trap—a meticulously woven web of deceit that had ensnared them all. The last suspect, the one who had promised vital clues, had led them straight into the lion's den. And now, Shepherd's hope, already hanging by a thread, threatened to unravel completely.

As he scanned the battlefield, Shepherd's heart sank. Bodies littered the ground, both gangsters and officers alike. The warehouse, once a haven for illegal activities, now stood as a testament to the brutal violence that had unfolded within its walls. The flickering lights overhead cast eerie shadows, turning the scene into a macabre dance of light and darkness.

Amidst the chaos, Shepherd's gaze fell upon the figure of the suspect, sprawled on the ground, clutching his bleeding leg. Pain etched across his face, he lay motionless, his consciousness lost to the shock. The scent of desperation clung to him, mingling with the stench of gun smoke.

Shepherd's footsteps echoed through the warehouse as he approached the fallen suspect. He knelt beside him, his gloved hand reaching out to check for a pulse. The suspect's heartbeat was faint, his breath shallow. Time was running out.

"Medic!" Shepherd's voice cut through the cacophony, laced with urgency. "We need a medic here, now!"

As the medics rushed to attend to the injured suspect, Shepherd's mind raced, trying to make sense of the situation. How had they fallen into this trap? Who was behind the elaborate deception? The answers eluded him, slipping through his fingers like smoke.

Just as Shepherd turned to gather his thoughts and rally his remaining team members, a voice sliced through the chaos—a voice he hadn't expected to hear. "Detective Shepherd, I presume?"

Shepherd's eyes snapped toward the sound, his gaze locking onto two figures standing at the entrance of the warehouse. They were impeccably dressed in tailored suits, exuding an air of authority. The woman, Sergeant Mary Copper, exuded confidence, her steely gaze fixed on Shepherd. Beside her stood Detective Captain Morgan Zap, a seasoned officer known for his unrelenting pursuit of justice.

Shepherd's blood ran cold. The arrival of Copper and Zap could only mean one thing: their squad, the Flying Squad, had been redeployed to take over the case. And the grounds for their arrival—sheer incompetence.

"Detective Shepherd," Copper's voice dripped with disdain. "It seems your team's mishandling of this case has forced our hand. The Sumter Police Department can no longer tolerate such incompetence."

Shepherd's jaw clenched, his fists tightening at his sides. The sting of their accusations struck deep, threatening to shatter the remnants of his shattered hope. He had given his all to this investigation, sacrificed sleep, and risked his life. And now, it was all being taken away from him.

"Give us the details," Zap's voice cut through the haze of despair that clouded Shepherd's mind. His words carried an air of authority, demanding answers and accountability.

Shepherd rose to his feet, his gaze steady, despite the turmoil within. "We were led here under false pretenses," he began, his voice tinged with a mix of frustration and determination. "The suspect we believed would provide crucial information turned out to be a puppet, manipulated by a cunning mastermind."

Copper's eyes narrowed, her skepticism evident. "And you fell for it? You led your team into a death trap?"

Shepherd's jaw tightened, a flicker of defiance crossing his features. "We had no reason to suspect deception. The evidence pointed in that direction, and our need for answers clouded our judgment. But make no mistake, there's a force at play here that goes far beyond what we initially thought."

Zap exchanged a meaningful glance with Copper, a silent understanding passing between them. "Tell us everything you know, Shepherd. We'll take it from here," Zap said, his tone laced with a mixture of authority and sympathy.

Shepherd hesitated for a moment, his mind grappling with conflicting emotions. Part of him resented the intrusion, the stripping away of his authority and the implication of failure. But another part recognized the opportunity it presented—a chance to bring justice to the victims, even if it meant relinquishing control.

Reluctantly, Shepherd began to recount the details of the investigation—the elusive clues, the dead ends, and the faint traces that had led them to this treacherous warehouse. He spared no detail, laying bare the complexity of the case, the stakes involved, and the relentless pursuit that had consumed his team. He'd also be turning in every single file as long as the case is concerned. He knew the new development would toil with his ego but he had no option.

Copper and Zap listened intently, their expressions morphing from skepticism to a mixture of surprise and concern. The gravity of the situation became clear as Shepherd's words unfolded, painting a picture of a shadowy criminal network that operated with precision and ruthlessness.

As the tale reached its conclusion, Shepherd's voice trailed off, his gaze fixed on the distant horizon. The warehouse, once a battleground, now lay in eerie silence—a testament to his team's perseverance and their ultimate defeat. But the spark of determination within him refused to be extinguished.

Copper and Zap exchanged another glance, a silent agreement passing between them. Copper's voice softened slightly as she spoke, her tone hinting at a newfound respect. "Shepherd, we understand the depth of your commitment. Despite the circumstances, you've shown unwavering dedication to this case. We'll need your insight, your knowledge, to put an end to this web of deception."

Shepherd's gaze locked with Copper's, a glimmer of hope rekindling within him. Perhaps this unexpected turn of events could be the catalyst for a fresh start, a renewed pursuit of justice. The path ahead remained uncertain, but the arrival of Copper and Zap offered a glimmer of hope—a chance to reclaim what had been lost.

Just as Shepherd opened his mouth to respond, the sound of a distant gunshot shattered the stillness. Instinct kicked in, and Shepherd's training propelled him forward, his senses on high alert. Copper and Zap, too, snapped into action, drawing their weapons in synchronized motion.

With a sense of urgency, Shepherd led the way, his instincts guiding him toward the sound of danger. The chapter had ended, but the story was far from over. In the midst of chaos and uncertainty, Detective Shepherd, Sergeant Copper, and Captain Zap would face their greatest challenge yet—a relentless pursuit of justice that would push them to their limits.

Leadership batons have changed yet, the battle remained indifferent. They had to put in more effort or they'd be more murders.

# CHAPTER 13

## Breathless

H  E MISSED THE FIRST. He can't miss it twice. Solace was in the sitting room of Mr. Simmons' apartment, his raiding eyes going over the acrylic landscape painting clutched to the wall adjacent to him. At least, admiring the painting before killing the owner won't sound too bad.

He didn't want to but after being given a two-day ultimatum, his hands were tight.

Again, his brain would remind him that he had been tasked with a gruesome mission—to end the life of a probation officer with a dark secret. The weight of his decision pressed heavily upon him, his hands trembling with a mix of anticipation and doubt.

As he pushed open the creaking bedroom door, the scent of stale air mingled with the acrid tang of fear. The hallway stretched before him, its faded wallpaper peeling, mirroring the decay that lay within the hearts of those who resided there. Solace's senses heightened, his gaze fixated on the door that concealed his unsuspecting prey.

Stepping into the apartment, the atmosphere grew thick with tension. The room was dimly lit, casting long shadows that danced across the worn-out furniture. Solace's eyes locked onto the figure seated in the armchair—Mr. Simmons. The man's face betrayed a weariness, as if burdened by the weight of his own secrets.

Solace approached, his steps cautious and deliberate. The air seemed to thicken with each passing moment, the scent of desperation mingling with the taste of regret. His hand tightened around the hilt of the zigzag dagger concealed within his jacket, its cold touch sending a shiver down his spine.

Mr. Simmons glanced up, a flicker of recognition in his eyes. Solace felt a surge of adrenaline coursing through his veins, urging him to complete the task he had been assigned. But as he neared, a wave of unease washed over him, eroding his resolve.

He looked into the eyes of the man before him, seeing the human behind the facade of guilt. In that moment, a spark of compassion ignited within Solace—a fleeting reminder of the humanity he thought he had lost. A hesitation, a doubt, and his grip on the dagger wavered.

The room fell into an eerie silence, broken only by the sound of their breaths intermingling. Solace's mind raced, his conscience grappling with the weight of his choices. He knew the consequences of failure, the wrath that awaited him if he disobeyed. But he also knew the irreparable damage that taking a life would inflict upon his own soul.

In a split-second decision, Solace altered his plan. With a swift motion, he redirected the blade, aiming for a non-lethal blow. The sound of the dagger piercing the air was drowned out by the gasp that escaped the target's lips as the blade found its mark—a shallow wound to the man's neck.

Pain flitted across the face, his body slumping forward as darkness claimed him. Solace acted swiftly, ensuring the man would remain unconscious and spared from the fate that had been intended for him. The room grew still once more, the tension dissipating as Solace's conflicting emotions battled within him.

He knew the truth—Walter, the organization—would soon discover his deviation from their orders. They would hunt him relentlessly, showing no mercy for his act of defiance. But at that moment, Solace couldn't bring himself to care. The scent of betrayal hung heavy in the air, but so too did the aroma of redemption.

With a determined resolve, Solace turned away from the motionless Mr. Simmons, his mind racing with thoughts of escape. He knew he couldn't return to the organization, and couldn't face the consequences of his actions. He would vanish into the night, leaving behind the life he had known, embarking on a journey to outwit his pursuers and find solace in the shadows.

Solace had made a choice—a choice that would lead him down a treacherous road, pursued by those he had once.

# CHAPTER 14

## Better Guns

T HE INTERROGATION ROOM BUZZED with tension as Detective Shepherd and Detective Morgan faced the revived suspect. The air hung heavy with the scent of stale coffee and nervous anticipation. Shepherd observed the suspect closely, his keen eyes dissecting every nuance of the man's body language.

The suspect, his face pale and beads of sweat glistening on his forehead, sat handcuffed to the metal table. A throbbing pain emanated from his injured leg, a reminder of the shootout that had landed him in custody. Shepherd's fingers itched for his own gun, a familiar weight that offered comfort in uncertain situations.

Detective Morgan leaned forward, her piercing gaze fixed upon the suspect. "You expect us to believe that you're responsible for all the murders?" he asked, his voice tinged with skepticism.

The suspect, a hint of defiance in his eyes, nodded confidently. "I've been watching, waiting," he replied. "I wanted them to pay for what they did to me. The system failed, so I took matters into my own hands."

They caught him at the scene of the most recent murder. It had the exact signature of the usual murders since Detective Hine. He pleaded guilty and claimed responsibility but the cop found it to be a cheap joke—one that is too hard to buy.

Shepherd's fingers tightened around the edge of the table, his mind racing with doubts. The suspect's confession seemed too convenient, too perfectly aligned with their investigation. He knew the dangers of tunnel vision, of blindly accepting the first narrative that presented itself.

Detective Morgan leaned back, crossing his arms. "You'll need to provide more than just words, my friend," he stated firmly. "We need evidence, a solid link connecting you to these crimes."

Actually, they were evidence. Gary Murdoch of the Forensic team confirmed the murderer to be left-handed and black-haired. The suspect had both qualities. But Detective Shepherd felt it was all a decoy.

The suspect smirked, a glimmer of arrogance dancing in his eyes. "Oh, I've got evidence," he sneered. "But you won't find it. Not unless you play by my rules."

Shepherd's senses sharpened, his instincts urging him to remain cautious. He knew the game being played—cat and mouse, a battle of wits where the truth lay hidden amidst layers of deception. He had encountered criminals who revealed in manipulating the truth, who delighted in leading investigators astray.

Detective Morgan leaned forward again, his voice firm but controlled. "We don't negotiate with criminals," he declared. "If you want to prove your claims, you'll have to do it the hard way."

The suspect's eyes narrowed, a hint of frustration flickering across his face. "You're making a mistake," he growled. "I could help you close this case, bring you the evidence you need. But you refuse to see reason."

Shepherd interjected, his voice measured. "We're not here to play games," he stated, his gaze locked with the suspect's. "If you truly have information that can help us, then speak. We're running out of time."

A flicker of doubt crossed the suspect's eyes, a momentary crack in his facade. "Fine," he relented, his voice tinged with frustration. "But remember, you asked for this."

With a calculated pause, the suspect launched into a detailed account of his alleged crimes. He described the methods, the victims, and even provided chilling details that sent shivers down Shepherd's spine. Every word seemed meticulously crafted, designed to elicit fear and establish his credibility.

But despite the suspect's convincing performance, Shepherd's instincts refused to let go of their skepticism. There was something off, a lingering doubt that clung to his mind like a stubborn shadow. He couldn't dismiss the nagging feeling that they were being led astray, that the true puppeteer remained concealed behind the scenes.

As the suspect concluded his account, Shepherd's mind raced with possibilities. The evidence, if it existed, would be the key to unraveling the truth. But with the suspect playing his dangerous game, the path forward remained treacherous and uncertain. Shepherd knew they couldn't afford to blindly trust the suspect's words. They needed solid proof, irrefutable evidence that would stand up in court.

Detective Morgan leaned back in her chair, his eyes fixed on Shepherd. "What do you think, Shepherd?" he asked, his voice laced with a hint of skepticism.

He didn't believe the suspect. Shepherd could hear it in his tone and see it in his gestures.

Shepherd met his gaze, his expression grave. "There's more to this than meets the eye," he replied, his voice low and steady. "His story sounds too polished, too convenient. I can't shake the feeling that we're being led down a treacherous path."

Morgan nodded, his eyes narrowing as she processed his words. "I feel it too," he admitted. "But we can't ignore his claims completely. We need to dig deeper, find the truth hidden beneath the layers of deception."

Silence enveloped the room as the weight of their predicament settled upon them. Shepherd's mind raced, searching for a way to navigate the treacherous maze they found themselves in. They needed a breakthrough, a new angle that would shed light on the suspect's true motives.

Suddenly, Shepherd's gaze fell upon a small, unassuming detail—the suspect's clenched fists. In that moment, an idea sparked in his mind, a daring plan that might just lead them closer to the truth.

"I have an idea," Shepherd said, his voice filled with determination. "Let's test his claims. Let's bring in the forensics team to thoroughly examine the crime scenes he mentioned. If his story holds up, we'll find evidence that corroborates his confession. If it doesn't, well, then we know he's been playing us all along."

Detective Morgan's eyes lit up with a mix of intrigue and caution. He recognized the risk involved, but he also knew that they couldn't afford to ignore any avenue that might bring them closer to the truth.

"Alright, Shepherd," he replied, her voice tinged with a hint of excitement. "Alright, get Gary Murdoch," he approved. Detective Shepherd was about shuffling through the door when he added. "But remember, we need to proceed with caution."

Shepherd nodded, a steely determination settling upon his shoulders. They had entered a dangerous game, one where the lines between truth and deception blurred. But he refused to let doubt consume him. He would uncover the hidden truths, expose the puppeteer pulling the strings, and bring justice to those who deserved it.

As they prepared to set their plan in motion, a sense of urgency filled the air. The scent of anticipation mingled with the lingering doubt, creating a potent mix that fueled their determination. They would unravel the mysteries that plagued their investigation, no matter the cost.

Detectives Shepherd and Morgan stood on the edge of their luck— the path ahead was treacherous. And with each step they took, they inched closer to the heart of a conspiracy that threatened to consume them both.

\*\*\*

The moon hung high in the night sky, casting an eerie glow over the city as Detective Shepherd and Detective Morgan moved with purpose through the dimly lit streets. The weight of their decision rested heavily upon them, their determination unwavering despite the looming danger.

As they made their way to the first crime scene mentioned by the suspect, Shepherd couldn't shake the feeling that they were being watched. The hair on the back of his neck stood on end, a primal instinct warning him of the lurking threat. He glanced at Morgan, his eyes scanning their surroundings with a mix of caution and anticipation.

The crime scene unfolded before them, a chilling tableau of violence and despair. Shepherd's senses heightened as he took in the scene—the acrid scent of dried blood, the chill of the night air seeping through his coat, and the eerie silence that hung in the deserted alleyway.

Their forensics team worked diligently, combing the area for any shred of evidence that would either validate or debunk the suspect's claims. Shepherd watched their every move, his eyes searching for the truth amidst the chaos. He knew that their next steps would determine the course of their investigation and, potentially, their lives.

Hours passed like an eternity as the team meticulously collected samples and documented their findings. Finally, as the first light of dawn began to break through the horizon, the forensic expert approached Shepherd and Morgan, a mix of disappointment and intrigue etched upon her face.

"We've found some traces of the suspect's DNA at the crime scene," Gary Murdoch announced, heis coarse baritone carrying a hint of uncertainty. "But it's not conclusive. There are also inconsistencies that raise doubts about the authenticity of his claims."

Shepherd's heart sank, a mixture of frustration and relief flooding through him. It seemed that his instincts had not failed him—the suspect's story was indeed a web of half-truths and manipulation.

Detective Morgan stepped forward, his gaze unwavering. "We can't let this setback deter us," he said, her voice steady. "We'll move on to the next lead on and continue our search for the truth."

With renewed determination, Shepherd and Morgan pressed on, their resolve unyielding. They delved into the dark sides of the county uncovering more crime scenes and dissecting each piece of evidence with a meticulous eye.

As they worked tirelessly, their pursuit of justice sent ripples through the criminal underworld. The organization, sensing their escalating threat, unleashed their own countermeasures. Shadows moved in the periphery, whispers of betrayal echoing through the ranks.

Detective Shepherd had reasons to give up but his resilience knew no boundaries. He acknowledged that the stakes were higher than he ever imagined. The city held its breath, waiting for the inevitable clash of wills—a clash that would determine the fate of not only Shepherd and Morgan, but also the fragile balance between justice and corruption.

In the shadows, a figure watched, biding their time, their intentions shrouded in darkness. And with each passing moment, the trap tightened, threatening to ensnare them all in a deadly embrace from which escape seemed impossible.

Then out of the blues, Detective Brown would ask a valid disturbing question.

"If the suspect's claims are wrong, who paid him to make them up?"

*Who's he working for?*

## CHAPTER 15

### In War with Flaws

R UNNING HAD NEVER BEEN easy. Solace felt he had done it. But, he got to the verge of flunking.

Solace's heart skipped a beat and his legs got frozen in the doorway of his motel room. The once-neat space had been transformed into a chaotic mess, a twisted reflection of the turmoil within his own mind.

Drawers were yanked open, their contents strewn across the floor like breadcrumbs leading to an unknown destination. The bed, once inviting and comforting, was now a jumble of torn sheets and overturned pillows. It was as if a tornado had ravaged his sanctuary, leaving behind only the remnants of a life on the run.

His eyes scanned the room, taking in every minute detail. The stale scent of fear hung heavy in the air, mingling with the acrid odor of torn pages from his journal. Solace moved cautiously, his fingertips tracing the edge of the dresser, searching for any clue that might explain the intrusion. His hands trembled, betraying the fear that threatened to consume him.

As he knelt to pick up a fallen photograph, Solace's eyes locked onto the image of a woman, her smile a bittersweet memory. His sister, Maria. The photograph had been taken years ago, before their lives had been torn apart. The touch of the photograph brought forth a flood of emotions, reminding him of the pain and guilt that had led him down this path.

A creaking floorboard shattered the silence, jolting Solace back to the present. He swiftly pocketed the photograph and reached for the small knife he kept hidden beneath his jacket. His senses heightened, he moved stealthily towards the sound, his heart racing with a mixture of anticipation and dread.

Peering around the corner, Solace's eyes widened as he caught sight of a figure rummaging through his belongings. The intruder was tall and imposing, his features hidden beneath a dark hood. Solace's mind raced, contemplating his next move. Should he confront the stranger or retreat, preserving what little safety remained?

The decision was made for him as the intruder turned abruptly, his eyes meeting Solace's with a cold intensity. "Well, well, if it isn't Solace, who would it be?" the figure sneered, his voice a venomous whisper.

Solace's grip tightened around the knife as he squared his shoulders, his voice steady despite the turmoil within. "Who are you?" he demanded, a flicker of defiance in his eyes.

"We've been looking for you," Solace!" the figure mumbled, tossing a dagger into the air as if for Solace to admire.

"I said who are you?" Solace barked, his tone grew louder and was ebbed with fury.

The intruder chuckled darkly, the sound sending a shiver down Solace's spine. "Call me Blackthorn," he replied, stepping forward with deliberate purpose. "And I'm here to make sure you pay for what you've done."

Solace's mind raced, searching for answers, for a way out of this deadly game. "I haven't done anything," he insisted, his voice tinged with desperation. "You've got the wrong person."

Blackthorn's laughter echoed through the room, bouncing off the walls like a haunting melody. "Oh, Solace, you were always good at playing the innocent, weren't you?" he taunted, his eyes narrowing in predatory delight. "But we know the truth. We know about Walter and his organization. And we know you're the key to bringing them down."

Solace's heart skipped a beat, the weight of betrayal heavy upon him. How had they found him? How much did they know? His mind raced, searching for a way to escape the clutches of Blackthorn and the mysterious organization he represented.

A sudden crash from the adjacent room shattered the tense standoff, drawing both men's attention. Solace's eyes darted to the source of the noise, a flicker of hope igniting within him. It was his chance, his chance to break free from the clutches of Blackthorn and whatever sinister web he was entangled in. Without a moment's hesitation, Solace lunged forward, using the distraction to his advantage. He swung his fist with all his might, catching Blackthorn off guard and sending him stumbling backward.

As Blackthorn struggled to regain his footing, Solace darted towards the open door, his heart pounding in his ears. He could hear Blackthorn's furious footsteps close behind him, the sound of their pursuit echoing through the dimly lit corridor. Solace's mind raced, his senses heightened, as he navigated the maze-like corridors of the motel, desperate to find an escape route.

The sharp smell of disinfectant assaulted Solace's nostrils as he sprinted down the stairs, his hand grazing the cold, metal railing for balance. He could feel the burn in his legs, the adrenaline pumping through his veins, propelling him forward. His senses were on high alert, every sound, every flicker of movement magnified in his mind.

Reaching the ground floor, Solace burst through the entrance, his lungs gasping for air as he darted into the cool night. The chilling wind cut through his clothes, raising goosebumps on his skin, but he paid no mind to the discomfort. He had to keep running, keep putting distance between himself and the relentless pursuit behind him.

Solace's eyes scanned the darkened streets, searching for a glimmer of safety. It was then that he spotted the flashing neon sign of a rundown diner a few blocks away. With a surge of hope, he sprinted towards it, his feet pounding against the pavement, the sound echoing in his ears.

He just frustrated the beastly assassin.

***

Pushing open the heavy door, Solace stumbled into the diner, his breath ragged. The scent of freshly brewed coffee and sizzling bacon enveloped him, providing a brief moment of respite from the chaos outside. The place was nearly empty, save for a few tired souls hunched over their plates, lost in their own thoughts.

Solace approached the counter, his hand trembling as he reached for the receiver of an old-fashioned payphone. He needed help, someone he could trust, someone who could help him unravel the truth behind Walter and his organization. As he dialed the familiar number, he couldn't help but feel a mix of relief and trepidation. Would they be able to help him? Or was he merely diving deeper into the abyss?

The phone rang, each shrill ring adding to the knot of anticipation in Solace's chest. Finally, a voice crackled through the line, filled with a mix of concern and urgency. "Solace? Is that you?" It was Maria, his sister, the only person he could truly rely on.

"Maria," Solace breathed, his voice laced with a mixture of relief and desperation. "I'm in trouble. I need your help."

There was a brief pause on the other end of the line, and then Maria's voice came through, steady and resolute. "Stay where you are, Solace. I'll come for you."

"Listen, Maria," Solace called, stopping her from snapping the telephone line. "Do not involve the cops in this!"

"I-I-just dialed 911…"

*Shit*

"Call them off, now. You'll never get to see me again if you come around with the cops," he said and hung up, not letting Maria agree to his terms or not.

As Solace hung up the phone, a shadowy figure slipped into the diner, unnoticed by the weary patrons. It was Blackthorn, a sinister grin on his face, his eyes gleaming with a predatory hunger. He had caught up with Solace once again, ready to deliver his own brand of justice.

*Son of a bitch. How did he find me?*

As Blackthorn took a menacing step forward, Solace's hand slid under his jacket, gripping the handle of the small knife concealed within. His fingers tightened around the weapon, its cold familiarity empowering him with a newfound resolve. He would defend himself, protect his sister, and ensure that justice prevailed.

Sensing the tension in the air, the few remaining customers glanced up from their meals, their gazes fixated on the unfolding confrontation. The sound of their hushed whispers mingled with the soft hum of the diner's background music, creating an eerie backdrop to the impending clash.

"You can't hide forever, Solace," Blackthorn growled, his voice dripping with malice. "We've come too far to let you slip through our fingers again."

Solace's eyes darted around the room, searching for any means of escape. He knew he had to buy time until Maria arrived, until they could face this dangerous adversary together. His heart hammered against his chest, the seconds ticking away like a countdown to his fate.

Without warning, Solace lunged forward, his knife gleaming in the dim light as he aimed it at Blackthorn's arm. The air crackled with tension as the blade sliced through the space, narrowly missing its intended target. A gasp escaped the onlookers' lips, their eyes widening in disbelief.

But Blackthorn was no ordinary adversary. He deftly sidestepped the attack, his movement's fluid and calculated. In one swift motion, he retaliated, striking Solace with a powerful blow to the ribs. Pain seared through Solace's body, momentarily disorienting him.

As Solace staggered backward, his vision blurred and his breath labored, a surge of determination surged within him. He couldn't let himself be defeated, not now. He had come too far to succumb to the shadows that threatened to consume him.

Solace grew more scared. He just caught the owner of the space making a call. It has to be the cop he's calling. He had to leave as soon as he could.

Summoning every ounce of strength, Solace rose to his feet, his eyes locking onto Blackthorn's menacing figure. "You won't win," he declared, his voice filled with a newfound resolve. "I won't let you destroy everything I've fought for."

Blackthorn smirked, his eyes gleaming with sadistic pleasure. "Oh, but I already have, Solace," he taunted, his words like venomous whispers. "Your fate was sealed the moment you chose to defy us."

As the standoff intensified, the diner's entrance swung open, a gust of wind billowing in. Maria stood at the threshold, her eyes ablaze with determination. "Leave him alone!" she commanded, her voice filled with a mixture of anger and protection.

Blackthorn's expression contorted into a snarl as he faced the unexpected arrival. Solace's heart swelled with relief at the sight of his sister, his ally in this treacherous game. But the danger was far from over.

Blackthorn might harm her.

A tense silence descended upon the room, broken only by the heavy breathing of the combatants. The onlookers held their breath, their eyes darting between the three figures poised for a final clash.

Suddenly, a deafening gunshot shattered the stillness, causing everyone to flinch in shock. Solace's eyes widened as pain erupted within him, a searing fire tearing through his chest. He staggered backward, clutching the wound, his vision fading into darkness.

Maria's scream pierced the air as time seemed to slow down. The echo of the gunshot reverberated through the diner, mingling with the collective gasps and cries of the patrons. Panic seized their hearts, the scent of fear now overpowering the aroma of coffee and food.

Maria's body hit the floor, his senses dulled by the excruciating pain radiating from her chest. She fought to keep her eyes open, desperate to catch a glimpse of her brother, to ensure his safety amidst the chaos.

Through the haze of her fading consciousness, Maria saw Solace's silhouette, his face etched with terror and grief. He knelt beside him, his trembling hands pressing against her wound in a futile attempt to stem the flow of blood. His voice trembled with tears as he whispered her name, his words a soothing melody in her ears as the fangs of death began intoxicating her.

But the world around them continued to unravel. Blackthorn, unfazed by the violence he had wrought, seized the opportunity to disappear into the shadows, leaving behind a trail of destruction and broken lives. Maria's grip on reality weakened, the edges of her vision blurring as darkness threatened to claim him.

"Stay with me, Maria," Solace pleaded, his voice desperate, as if defying the inevitable. "We'll find help. We'll get through this."

Maria tried to respond, to reassure him, but her strength waned with every passing moment. The pain intensified, becoming an all-consuming fire that gnawed at his very core. As her eyelids grew heavy, he managed to utter a final, rasping breath. "Keep fighting... Solace..."

With those words, Maria surrendered to the darkness, her body limp and lifeless. The scent of blood mingled with the fragrant residue of shattered dreams, and the diner transformed into a grim tableau of tragedy.

Solace's cries echoed through the desolate space, the sound a mournful symphony of loss. He clutched Solace's lifeless form, his fingers stained crimson, tears streaming down her face. In his eyes burned a fierce determination, an unyielding resolve to avenge his sister and shatter the man who took her life

In the midst of grief and turmoil, the seeds of justice took root. Solace, burdened with a pain that could never be fully extinguished, would rise from the ashes of tragedy and pursue the answers he sought. He would become the beacon of light that dispelled the shadows of betrayal, fighting not only for her sister but for all those entangled in the web of darkness.

As Solace's cradled lifeless Maria's body, vowing to carry on his legacy, a glimmer of hope pierced through the shroud of despair. The battle was far from over. The war with flaws had claimed its first casualty, igniting a fire within Maria that would burn brighter and fiercer than ever before.

And so, as the sirens wailed in the distance, their mournful cry harmonized with Solace's grief-stricken cries. He never wants them to be seen by the cops.

The stage was set for a reckoning, and the forces that had conspired to silence Solace would soon discover that his legacy, his indomitable spirit, would endure, casting a long and unforgiving shadow upon those who dared to stand in the way of justice.

Staggeringly, he'd cup Maria's lifeless body and dogtrot into the dark, his eyes soaked with tears and pain.

## CHAPTER 16

## Torpedoes

D ETECTIVE MORGAN SAT AT HIS DESK, poring over the reports from the failed assassination attempt on the probation officer at Benton Ridge. Two days had passed since the incident, and the realization that he had only just learned of it gnawed at him. His gaze shifted to the evidence experts bustling around the apartment, carefully collecting every trace that could lead to the perpetrator.

After what seemed like an eternity, the team emerged, their faces etched with seriousness. The lead investigator approached Detective Morgan with a file in hand. "We've searched the apartment thoroughly, sir," he reported. "No stone was left unturned."

Detective Morgan nodded, his eyes scanning the file. "What did you find?"

"Forensics recovered a partial fingerprint on a doorknob," the investigator explained. "It doesn't match anyone in our database, but it's a significant lead."

His curiosity piqued, Detective Morgan made his way to the interrogation room where the attack victim, the probation officer, sat waiting. The room exuded an air of tension, the walls seemingly holding the weight of unspoken secrets. As he entered, he observed the man's physical state—a mix of exhaustion, fear, and relief at having survived the attempt on his life.

"Thank you for coming in Mr. Simmons," Detective Morgan began, his voice calm yet authoritative. "I understand you've been through a traumatic experience. We're here to help."

Mr. Simmons nodded, his gaze meeting the detective's with a mixture of vulnerability and determination. "I never expected something like this to happen," he admitted, his voice tinged with fear. "But I'm grateful to be alive."

Detective Morgan leaned forward, his eyes piercing. "I need you to think back to the moment of the attack," he said. "Was there anything peculiar about it? Any detail that stood out?"

The probation officer hesitated for a moment, his brow furrowing as he recalled the events. "Yes," he finally replied, his voice tinged with uncertainty. "It felt... strange. The assailant had the perfect opportunity to finish me off, but he deliberately left me alive."

Detective Morgan's eyebrows shot up in surprise. "Intentionally?" he questioned, a sense of intrigue tingling in the back of his mind.

The probation officer nodded, his expression filled with confusion. "Yes. It was as if he wanted me to know that they had the power to end my life but chose not to," the man explained, splaying his hands in innocence.

The detective's mind raced, contemplating the significance of this revelation. Who would want to send such a message? And why spare the life of their target? As he delved deeper into his thoughts, a sense of urgency pierced the room.

Suddenly, Detective Mary burst into the room, her face etched with concern. "Emergency, Morgan!" she exclaimed, breathless. "There's been another murder. We need you at the scene immediately."

Detective Morgan's heart skipped a beat. Another murder so soon after the failed assassination attempt could only mean one thing—the shadow of darkness loomed closer than ever. He stood up swiftly, leaving the probation officer behind, his mind now consumed by the urgency of the new case.

***

Racing to the crime scene, Detective Morgan's senses were heightened. The stench of death hung heavy in the air, mingling with the metallic tang of blood. Blue and red lights bathed the street, casting an eerie glow upon the macabre tableau before him.

As he approached the scene, Detective Shepherd, his partner, met him with a grave expression. "It's a brutal one, Morgan," he said, his voice filled with a mixture of concern and determination. "The victim was killed less than two hours ago. The scene is gruesome, and it appears to be the work of a skilled and ruthless killer."

Detective Morgan took a deep breath, preparing himself for what lay ahead. The sight that awaited him was as chilling as it was perplexing. The victim, a middle-aged man, lay sprawled on the ground, his lifeless eyes staring into the void. The crimson pool surrounding him contrasted starkly with the muted tones of the urban landscape.

The head of forensics approached Detective Morgan, a small film canister in hand. "Detective," he began, his voice laced with urgency, "we found multiple fingerprints at the scene, all belonging to the same person."

Detective Morgan's eyes narrowed as he took the film canister, his hands trembling slightly with anticipation. Inside lay the key to unraveling the mysteries that shrouded this case—the identity of the killer. He knew the moment he opened it, a new path would reveal itself, leading him closer to the truth.

Carefully extracting the film, Detective Morgan studied it under a nearby streetlight. The multiple fingerprints were clear and distinct, forming a pattern that was etched into his memory. And then, his heart skipped a beat.

His eyes widened in disbelief as the name registered in his mind—Templar Solace. It was a name he had come across before, a name that now resurfaced like a haunting specter in his investigation. The connection to Morris Lodge sent a shiver down his spine.

A mix of confusion and determination surged within Detective Morgan. How was it possible that the fingerprints of Templar Solace, the man they had been hunting, were now found at the scene of this fresh murder? The web of deception had grown intricate, entangling their lives in a complex dance of shadows and secrets.

As he turned to Detective Shepherd, their eyes met, a shared understanding passing between them. The battle against darkness had taken an unexpected turn. The hunt for Templar Solace had become more urgent, and the line between hunter and hunted blurred in the face of an enigmatic foe.

"We need to find Templar Solace," Detective Morgan declared, his voice laced with a mix of determination and unease. "He's at the center of this web, and we must unravel the truth behind his involvement."

Detective Shepherd nodded, his gaze unwavering. "What's at stake? ," he asked, his voice resonating with a resolute resolve. "He might be the actual danger."

"Hop in," Detective Mary charged at Shepherd, nodding to the car.

As they prepared to embark on the hunt for Templar Solace, a realization washed over Detective Morgan—a chilling thought that sent a shiver down his spine. The connection between the failed assassination attempt and the fresh murder painted a picture of calculated manipulation, of an intricate plan woven by a mastermind.

In the darkness of the night, as they ventured deeper into wherever the search for Solace could lead them, Detective Morgan knew that the answers they sought were just beyond their reach. The scent of danger lingered in the air, mingling with the anticipation of the unknown. The hunt for Templar Solace would lead them down treacherous paths, testing their resolve and pushing their limits.

With the fingerprints of their elusive target in hand, Detective Morgan and his team set out, determined to unravel the mysteries that entangled their lives. The pursuit of justice had taken a new form, and the stakes had never been higher.

The hunt for Templar Solace had only just begun, and the county held its breath, unaware of the imminent danger that lurked in its midst. Detective Morgan and his team tirelessly pursued leads, connecting the intricate threads of the conspiracy that had ensnared them.

They shared his pictures. Gave his description. Made him a general concern. Chief Siren gave a week's interval to place a bounty on him after he was declared wanted.

Detectives Morgan, Shepherd and Mary took no chances. The fearless cops pieced together fragments of evidence, interrogated witnesses, and pursued every possible lead. Each step forward brought them closer to Templar Solace, the brain behind their nightmares.

Meanwhile, the county teetered on the edge of chaos. The shadow of fear loomed over its inhabitants, their senses heightened by the knowledge that a cunning killer remained at large. Whispers of Solace's name circulated through the streets, evoking a mix of curiosity, dread, and speculation.

Detective Morgan found himself drawn deeper into the enigma surrounding Templar Solace. He scoured the files, his eyes scanning the evidence, desperate to uncover the truth that eluded them. The scent of old case files filled the air, mingling with the faint smell of coffee that permeated the precinct, fueling their relentless pursuit.

\*\*\*

On a Friday, as the sun dipped below the horizon, casting long shadows over Sumter County, Detective Morgan received an urgent call. Another murder occurred—an act of calculated brutality that mirrored the killer's previous pattern. The weight of the news hung heavy in the detective's chest, a cold reminder of the evil they were up against.

Without hesitation, Detective Morgan and his team rushed to the scene. The air was thick with tension, the crime scene alive with the dance of flashing lights and the hum of whispered conversations. The victim, a young woman, lay lifeless, her body a canvas of violence. The sight stirred a mix of anger and determination within the detective.

As he approached the scene, Detective Shepherd, his trusted partner, handed him a small envelope. "Forensics discovered something significant," he said, his voice grave. "These fingerprints were found at the crime scene. It's a match to Templar Solace."

Again. It was Templar Solace.

Detective Morgan's heart raced, his mind racing to make sense of the pieces falling into place. The realization struck him with a force that left him momentarily breathless. Solace's involvement in this murder solidified the understanding that he was not merely a pawn but a calculated mastermind, leaving his twisted signature on every crime scene.

The detective's grip tightened on the envelope, his fingers tracing the edges, a surge of determination flowing through him. The chase had intensified, and they were closing in on the puppeteer of darkness. But the question remained—what was the motive behind these killings? And why did Solace deliberately leave survivors?

As the city slept, unaware of the impending storm, Detective Morgan vowed to unveil the secrets that shrouded Templar Solace. His mind buzzed with unanswered questions, a relentless pursuit for justice fueling his every step.

As the night unfolded, casting its inky cloak over the county, Detective Morgan's resolve grew unyielding. With the fingerprints in his possession and a renewed sense of purpose burning in his eyes, he took a deep breath, ready to face the darkness that awaited him.

The hunt for Templar Solace had brought them clear hope. Answers were now within reach. But what lay ahead remained a mystery.

As Detective Shepherd lay down in sleep, his heart whispered:

*Who is he killing tonight?*

# CHAPTER 17

## Murderers Murderer

W ALTER'S EYES SHOT OPEN, greeted by the cold barrel of a gun pressed firmly against his forehead. The dim light of the bedroom cast sinister shadows, amplifying the gravity of the situation. It was the first time Solace had ever seen him look terrified. Solace stood there, his face a mask of determination, as he held the gun steady, never breaking eye contact.

"Walter," Solace's voice was low and laced with bitterness, "we need to talk about what you never mentioned."

Walter's mind raced, trying to comprehend the sudden turn of events. How had Solace found out? How long had he known? The weight of guilt bore down on Walter's chest, making it difficult to breathe. Solace knew secrets he had carefully guarded, secrets that could shatter everything he had built.

"I...I don't know what you're talking about," Walter stammered, desperately grasping for a way out.

Solace, unrelenting, reached into his pocket and retrieved a small device. He pressed a button, and the room was filled with the crackling sound of a voice recording. The voice was unmistakably Walter's, engaged in a conversation that he had believed to be buried in the depths of darkness.

It was the night a couple had been viciously attacked and murdered, their lives stolen for an ancient European sculptor. A piece that was destined for a national museum, a priceless artifact worth millions of dollars. The guilt weighed heavily on Walter's conscience, knowing he had orchestrated the whole affair.

In the recording, a police officer's voice trembled with fear, desperately bargaining for his life. The agreement was clear—Walter would keep his share of the proceeds from the antique deal in exchange for sparing the officer's life. The cold, calculating nature of Walter's voice sent shivers down Solace's spine.

*Police officer: That was way out of context. We never agreed on a murders. No blood was supposed to be shed.*

*Walter: But it happened.*

*Police Officer: It could be avoided. You ordered your men to take laws into their hands.*

*Walter: In Sumter, we are the law.*

*Police Officer: Spare me that, you jerk. Listen, you breached our agreement. You did the unacceptable and they will come all out for you.*

*Walter: Who are they?*

*Police Officer: The Police, the Council, their family…nature will come after you, Tyndale.*

*Walter: Sometimes, mistakes are inevitable my dear Service Medalist. We can't cry over spilled milk. You'll get your share of the cake in a few days.*

*Police Officer: You've got to be kidding me. You think I'm that cruel. All we wanted was the antique. That god-damned antique and not the lives of an innocent family.*

*Walter: Stop ranting like an old hungry woman and wait for your share off the deal!*

*Police Officer: Listen to this, Tyndale. I do not want to be in any way affiliated to that inhumane act. Keep the money. Keep the antique. But, most importantly, keep my family out of this.*

*Walter: Ray…ray…ray…*

The telephone line snapped.

"They were all I had," Solace's voice wavered with a mix of sorrow and anger, "but you killed them in one night!"

Solace raised the gun and without hesitation, fired a single shot. Pain exploded through Walter's leg as he crumpled to the ground, gasping for breath. The room spun around him, and the metallic scent of blood filled his nostrils. The physical agony only intensified the weight of guilt that threatened to consume him.

Solace stood over Walter, his eyes filled with a mixture of anguish and fury. "You were my friend, Walter. I trusted you, and you threw it all away for greed."

Walter, fighting through the pain, managed to lock eyes with Solace. "I did what I had to do. You don't understand."

Solace's grip on the gun tightened, his voice laced with disappointment. "No, Walter, you're the one who doesn't understand. Loyalty, friendship—those are the things that matter. You abandoned them all."

As the room swayed around him, Walter reached out, desperately grasping for any thread of redemption. "Solace, please... There's still a way we can fix this. We can make things right."

Solace's face twisted into a bitter smile. "Make things right? There's no going back, Walter. You crossed a line that can't be uncrossed."

The room fell silent, save for the sound of Walter's labored breathing. The pain in his leg radiated through his body, but it paled in comparison to the ache in his heart. He had let down the only person he considered family, and now he would pay the price.

Solace took a step back, his eyes filled with a mixture of sorrow and determination. "I won't kill you, Walter. Not yet. A flicker of relief washed over Walter's face, his eyes searching Solace's for a glimmer of mercy. Solace, however, remained resolute, his voice cold and detached.

"But don't mistake my mercy for forgiveness," Solace warned, his voice slicing through the tension. "You will suffer, Walter. Just as you made others suffer."

Solace turned away, leaving Walter sprawled on the floor, his pain and regret consuming him. He limped towards the window, drawing back the heavy curtains to reveal the night sky. The moon hung high, casting an eerie glow over the city below.

"You have until sunrise," Solace declared, his voice filled with finality. "Before the dawn breaks, you will tell me everything. Every secret you've hidden, every deception you've woven. And if you don't... Well, let's just say the consequences will be far worse than a bullet in the leg."

Walter's breath hitched as fear gripped him once again. He had underestimated Solace, his own hubris blinding him to the depths of his friend's anger. With each passing moment, the weight of his betrayal grew heavier.

Solace's silhouette loomed against the moonlit backdrop, his voice a chilling whisper. "Remember, Walter, the council will know. They will see you for what you truly are."

With that, Solace vanished into the night, leaving Walter alone with his pain and his secrets. The room closed in on him, its walls seeming to tighten around him like a prison. The stench of blood mingled with the musty scent of fear, creating an oppressive atmosphere that clung to him.

Walter dragged himself across the floor, using every ounce of strength to reach his desk. His trembling hand fumbled for his phone, the device that held the key to his darkest secrets. Sweat coated his forehead as he dialed a number, hoping for a lifeline, for someone who could help him salvage what was left.

The line crackled to life, and a voice filled with venom answered on the other end. "Walter, you've got a lot of nerve calling me."

"Wesley," Walter croaked, his voice thick with desperation. "I need your help. Solace knows everything. He's going to expose me to the council."

A low chuckle reverberated through the phone, sending a shiver down Walter's spine. "Well, well, looks like the mighty Walter has fallen. Tell me, what's in it for me if I help you?"

Walter's heart sank, realizing he was at the mercy of a man even more ruthless than himself. He had no choice but to play his last card.

"Wesley, the antique—the one we stole. It's hidden in a warehouse by the docks. Worth millions. Help me, and you can have it all."

There was a brief silence on the other end, as if Wesley was weighing his options. Walter held his breath, hoping that greed would triumph over vengeance.

"Fine," Wesley finally replied, his voice dripping with malice. "But remember, Walter, you owe me. And I always collect my debts."

The line went dead, leaving Walter alone in the darkness, his fate hanging in the balance. He knew that he was walking a treacherous path, one that would only lead to more bloodshed and betrayal. But he had no other choice. He had to protect what little remained of his empire, no matter the cost.

As the first rays of dawn began to paint the sky in shades of orange and pink, Walter knew that time was running out. Solace would return, and the reckoning would begin. He had to gather his strength, face his demons, and hope that he could somehow regain control of the unraveling situation.

With a surge of determination, Walter pushed himself up from the floor, wincing as pain shot through his injured leg. He hobbled towards the wardrobe, reaching for a concealed compartment at the back. His trembling fingers found solace in the touch of cold steel—a compact pistol, his last line of defense.

As he secured the weapon in the waistband of his pants, a bitter taste filled his mouth, a stark reminder of the bitter choices he had made. The tang of regret mingled with the metallic scent of his own blood, further fueling his resolve. He couldn't let everything he had built crumble to dust.

The rising sun painted the room in a soft glow as Walter made his way to the study, where he had kept meticulous records of his illicit activities. He knew that Solace would demand answers, and he had to be prepared.

The room felt suffocating, the air thick with the weight of deceit.

Walter's eyes swept across the shelves lined with ancient tomes and artifacts, each holding secrets of their own. He reached for a weathered journal, its leather cover worn from years of use. Flipping through its pages, he found the details of every transaction, every dirty deal that had propelled him to power.

That was the key to his condemnation. He must set it ablaze before Solace's return.

***

The sound of a key turning in the front door lock sent a jolt of panic through Walter's veins. Solace had returned, and there was no turning back now. He pocketed the journal, tucking away his sins for the moment, and braced himself for the confrontation that awaited.

Solace strode into the study, his eyes burning with an intensity that sent a shiver down Walter's spine. The room seemed to darken as their gazes locked, the air charged with an electric tension. This was the moment of reckoning, where their twisted bond would be tested to its limits.

"You have until now to come clean," Solace's voice held a raw edge, the tone a mix of anger and sorrow. "No more lies, no more deception. Tell me everything."

Walter's heart pounded in his chest, his palms sweaty as he met Solace's unwavering gaze. With each passing second, the scent of desperation grew stronger, mingling with the fading aroma of the morning coffee that still lingered in the air.

Taking a deep breath, Walter began to speak, his voice laced with remorse and calculated honesty. He revealed the depths of his betrayal, his secret trades, and the lives he had sacrificed for his own gain. The words spilled forth, leaving a bitter taste on his tongue, as he exposed the darkness that had consumed him.

Solace listened in silence, his eyes searching for any flicker of truth amidst the sea of deceit. The room felt heavy, suffocating, as the weight of Walter's confession settled upon them. It was a battle between loyalty and vengeance, and the outcome would forever alter the course of their lives.

As Walter's voice trailed off, an eerie silence enveloped the room. Solace's face contorted with conflicting emotions, his grip tightening on the edge of the desk. A single tear slipped down his cheek, mingling with the beads of perspiration on his temple.

"I... I never thought it would come to this," Solace's voice quivered, his eyes reflecting a mix of sorrow and rage. "You were my brother, Walter. We were supposed to protect each other, not tear each other apart."

Walter's heart sank as the reality of his actions settled upon him. He had shattered the trust that had been forged through years of camaraderie, replaced it with greed and manipulation. The pain of his own betrayal cut deeper than any bullet wound ever could.

*What a world!*

# CHAPTER 18

## Worms

LOST IN AN ALLEY, YET AGAIN. Detectives Morgan and Shepherd stood at the entrance of a pitch dark alley, their hearts in their mouths and their guns trained forward.

The stranger's cryptic instructions had led them here, mentioning the name that had been haunting their investigation—Templar Solace. Intrigued yet wary, they followed the trail, driven by a desire to uncover the truth behind the figure's involvement in the murders that had plagued Sumter County.

The alley stretched before them, an abyss of shadows and hidden secrets. The scent of dampness and decay clung to the air, mingling with the distant whiff of cigarette smoke. Every step echoed with a hollow sound, reverberating off the graffiti-stained walls.

As they cautiously ventured deeper into the darkness, their flashlights casting erratic beams of light, a sight caught their attention—a lone swivel chair positioned in the center of the alley. Its presence seemed out of place, a peculiar beacon drawing them closer.

Detective Shepherd's hand instinctively moved towards the grip of his holstered gun, a silent reminder of the dangers that lurked in the shadows. Detective Morgan's gaze narrowed, his eyes scanning their surroundings for any signs of danger.

Approaching the chair, Shepherd's heart quickened as he noticed a briefcase resting upon its seat. The sight of it sent a shiver down his spine, a mixture of anticipation and caution intertwining within him.

"Careful, Shepherd," Morgan warned, his voice low and steady. "This could be a trap. Stay alert."

Shepherd nodded, his fingertips grazing the cold metal of the briefcase's handle. With a deep breath, he unlatched it, revealing its contents. But instead of valuable evidence or a vital clue, all he found were stacks of old newspapers, their pages yellowed with age and faded ink.

Frustration tinged with confusion washed over Shepherd as he sifted through the papers. The scent of old print filled his nostrils, a testament to the passage of time. The touch of delicate newsprint crinkled beneath his fingers, a physical connection to a bygone era.

Morgan's eyes narrowed as he caught sight of something hidden within the papers—a small flash drive, inconspicuous and easily overlooked. Shepherd plucked it from its hiding place, a flicker of anticipation igniting within him.

"This could be what they wanted us to find—a flashdrive," Shepherd murmured, his voice laden with a mix of curiosity and skepticism. "But what does it hold? And who would want to link us to these powerful clues?"

Morgan's gaze met Shepherd's, a shared determination burning in their eyes. "There's only one way to find out."

As they retraced their steps, the alley seemed to come alive with whispers of secrets and unspoken truths. The scent of mystery clung to their clothes, mingling with the musty odor of the newspapers. They knew that the path they were on would lead them to the heart of the darkness, where powerful forces conspired to hide the truth.

***

Back at the Sumter County Police Department, the two detectives settled into Morgan's office, the room enveloped in an air of anticipation. Shepherd connected the flash drive to the computer, the soft hum of technology filling the silence.

A flurry of images and documents appeared on the screen, a puzzle waiting to be solved. The sight of familiar faces, classified files, and hidden transactions hinted at a grand conspiracy that reached far beyond their initial investigations.

But just as they began to delve deeper into the digital labyrinth, the office door swung open with a forceful thud. A stern-faced captain stood in the doorway, his eyes narrowed with suspicion. The scent of authority mixed with an undercurrent of apprehension hung heavy in the room.

"What are you two doing?" the captain demanded, his voice sharp and authoritative. "Why are you tampering with evidence without proper authorization?"

Shepherd and Morgan exchanged a quick glance, their minds racing to come up with an explanation. They knew they had stumbled upon something significant, something that could potentially expose a web of corruption, but they hadn't anticipated their actions being scrutinized so quickly. That wasn't supposed to be a problem to any cop who dearly wished to put an end to the serial killings tearing Sumter County apart.

"Captain, we... we found this flash drive during our investigation," Shepherd replied, his voice steady yet tinged with caution. "We believe it may contain crucial information related to the recent murders and the ongoing corruption within the department."

The captain's eyes flickered with a mix of anger and concern. He stepped forward, his presence commanding the room. "Detectives, this is a dangerous path you're treading. You have no idea of the forces at play here. It's not your place to uncover the truth."

Morgan's brows furrowed, his voice laced with determination. "Captain, with all due respect, we cannot turn a blind eye to the corruption festering within our own ranks. Lives are at stake, and we believe that this investigation has ties to powerful figures."

The captain's gaze hardened, his fingers tapping impatiently against his side. "You're skating on thin ice, detectives. There are powers at play that you couldn't possibly comprehend."

Shepherd's grip tightened around the flash drive, his resolve unwavering. "Captain, we understand the risks, but we cannot stand idly by while innocent lives are destroyed. We have a duty to pursue justice, no matter the consequences."

A tense silence filled the room as the captain's gaze bore into them. The smell of uncertainty permeated the air, mixing with the metallic tang of determination. Finally, the captain let out a resigned sigh.

"You leave me no choice," he muttered, his voice laced with a mixture of disappointment and resignation. "I will have to report your actions to Internal Affairs. They will conduct their own investigation."

Shepherd and Morgan exchanged a glance, their eyes reflecting a silent understanding. They knew the risks they were taking, but they also knew that the truth had to be brought to light, no matter the cost.

As the captain turned to leave, Shepherd's voice cut through the air. "Captain, one thing remains clear—we will not rest until we uncover the full extent of this corruption. And if we find evidence of your involvement, we will not hesitate to bring you to justice as well."

The captain froze in his tracks, his back rigid. A flicker of unease passed over his face before he turned to face them, his expression unreadable.

"You're playing with fire, detectives," he warned, his voice dripping with a newfound coldness. "Be careful what you wish for."

With that ominous message hanging in the air, the captain exited the room, leaving Shepherd and Morgan to face the storm that awaited them. They knew their investigation had now entered a perilous phase, where the line between friend and foe blurred, and trust became a luxury they could no longer afford.

*But, how did he know they had the flashdrive?*

\*\*\*

Of all the information compressed into the flashdrive, only one came off valuable. It was a voice recording. Detective Shepherd could say how but the recording was tapped from a telephone conversation between the two men.

Detective Morgan first confirmed the second sound to be familiar but Shepherd had a strong intuition to take things slowly.

Tension hung on the air and silence became a deafening noise that went as far as their auricles. They were about to go down into the depths of revelations that'd put a full-blown stop to the nightmare they've been chasing for months—day and night, amid rain and sunshine.

The next file in the flashdrive they'd have made good use of was the CCTV footage but the captured photographs were too blurred and badly taken to be useful.

Sergeant Humphrey of the Informatics Unit spearheaded the raid of the flashdrive under the eagle-eyed scrutiny of Detectives Morgan and Shepherd. Detective Mary Copper slumped atop the swivel at the corner of the office. Chief Siren was on his way to the office too.

Tingles made it to the heart of every cop in the room as the sound of the recording popped into the air. It was slightly affected by signal interference but when connected to a twin-set loudspeaker, the conversation was audible enough to be heard and understood without craning one's ear.

*Policeman: I thought his murder was supposed to be it!*

*Man: It was only a grand opening.*

*Policeman: What the fuck do you mean by grand opening?*

*Man: You don't make our rules remember, you only stick to them*

*Policeman: You are overstepping the agreement, dammit. Don't you get it? He had what you needed. You took him with what you needed. So why more murders?*

*Man: Our Service Medalist wasn't a one-man-squad.*

The mention of one-man-squad was the statement that ushered Chief Siren into the room. He probably overheard it on his way in. The Chief slumped into the leather-quilted armchair and kept listening to the all-important information they've always wanted.

Man: *Real deals are sealed by real men and every real man on that deal mustn't live with what he knows.*

Policeman: *Including a gardener, Tyndale. A god-damned gardener?*

Man: *(He laughed hysterically). That was what he wanted you fools who are allowed to openly carry guns around to believe. You know no one!*

Policeman: *I don't care about what you think I know but the more you do this, the deadlier it gets. Not for me, you know. But for you, your men, your organization.*

Man: *(Another hard laugh). The last fun I had was when you all took away what I toiled for. You see this? It's fun for me. The more men down, the more safe our secrets. The safer you are too, my dear cop!*

Policeman: *I'm safe with or without you. I'm a cop*

Man: *One who pays loyalty to anti-police like me? Huh!*

*Policeman: I've got a family to protect, Tyndale. Think about that.*

*Man: I've got even more to protect, Detective.*

*Policeman: I've made myself close. I quit!*

*Man: (Laughs hysterically again). 1412 Nelson Street. A beautiful wife. Two smart boys. I know where they live, Detective.*

The policeman paused and gasped for breath.

*Policeman: Take my family out of this. We agreed to keep this between us.*

*Man: I know all my agreements. Every word of it. That's why they must be written and sealed. But, you are useless when you think you wanna play me.*

*Policeman: What do you want?*

*Man: You know what I want*

*Policeman: I can't do that.*

*Man: Get the stubborn cop into the warehouse tonight or meet your family at Olive Boulevard train station tomorrow morning.*

*Policeman: But I..You there, Tyndale. Shit!*

Chief Siren turned to Detective Morgan. 1412 Nelson Street. Get me Morgan Patterson, now.

# CHAPTER 19

## MacPherson Alley

A LLEYS BECAME THEIR ALLIES. This time, it was MacPherson Alley. Detective Morgan stepped cautiously into the. Detective Shepherd followed close behind, their eyes scanning the surroundings for any sign of the mysterious stranger who had lured them here. The sound of their footsteps echoed off the walls, heightening the tension in the air.

As they approached the swivel chair, Detective Shepherd's grip tightened on his sidearm. The chair stood eerily still, its worn leather creaking under the weight of anticipation. With a nod from Morgan, he slowly circled around it, his senses on high alert. His fingers brushed against the backrest, and he recoiled, feeling a faint stickiness on his skin.

Morgan moved closer, shining her flashlight on the chair. There, splattered across the leather, were dried crimson droplets, a macabre testament to the violence that had transpired. The metallic tang of blood reached her nostrils, mingling with the stench of decay that pervaded the alley.

A voice, low and gravelly, cut through the darkness. "Impressive, isn't it? How a single name can lead you down this treacherous path."

Morgan and Shepherd turned towards the sound, their eyes narrowing as they faced a figure emerging from the shadows. He was tall and imposing, his face hidden beneath a hat pulled low. The stranger's voice dripped with a mix of amusement and malice, sending shivers down their spines.

"Who are you?" Morgan demanded, his initially steady voice cracky but laced with boldness.

The stranger chuckled darkly. "Answers, my dear detectives. Answers to questions you haven't even begun to ask. But first, let's see if you're up to the challenge."

He gestured towards the briefcase on the swivel chair, its sleek black exterior beckoning them closer. Shepherd cautiously approached it, his gloved hand reaching out to grasp the handle. The case felt surprisingly light as he popped it open, revealing a treasure trove of newspapers meticulously arranged inside.

"These newspapers hold the key to the puzzle you seek," the stranger proclaimed, his voice dripping with intrigue. "But beware, not everything is as it seems."

Morgan's eyes darted over the headlines, his mind racing to make connections. He scanned the pages, each one revealing the haunting tales of crime and corruption that had plagued the county. As he delved deeper, his fingers brushed against something unexpected—a small flash drive hidden among the newsprint.

Again. Another flashdrive.

Shepherd withdrew the flash drive, a sense of foreboding settling in his gut. "What's on here?" he asked, his gaze fixed on the stranger.

"All the answers you seek, Detective Shepherd," the stranger replied with a wicked smile. "But be careful. The truth can be a dangerous thing."

Morgan's fingers tingled with anticipation as he reached for the flash drive. His pulse quickened, and a chill ran down the edge of his spine. With a glance exchanged between the two detectives, he plugged it into his laptop, the soft hum of the machine filling the silence.

As the screen flickered to life, images and documents appeared, revealing a web of intrigue that stretched far beyond what they had anticipated. The truth unfolded before their eyes—corrupt officials, hidden alliances, and the name that haunted their investigation, Templar Solace.

"The fingerprints," Shepherd murmured, his eyes widening in realization. "Templar Solace was present at both crime scenes. But why?"

The stranger's laughter cut through their thoughts, a chilling sound that echoed off the walls of the alley. "Ah, the invisible Templar Solace. A pawn in a much larger game," my dear detectives. Morgan's eyes narrowed, his determination resolute. "Tell us, then. Who is pulling the strings? Why are they targeting Templar Solace?"

The stranger took a step closer, the faint glow of the laptop casting ominous shadows across his face. "Patience, Detectives. All will be revealed in due time. But remember, curiosity can be a dangerous ally."

Shepherd clenched his fists, frustration building within him. "We're not pawns in your game. We need answers, and we won't rest until we get them."

The stranger's smile grew wider, a glimmer of admiration in his eyes. "Very well, Detectives. I can see the fire in your hearts. But be warned, the path you're on is treacherous. Dark forces are at play, and crossing them may cost you more than you can bear."

Morgan's voice held a steely resolve. "We've faced danger before. Even more gravy than this. We'll face it again. Tell us what we need to know."

The stranger's gaze flickered to the laptop screen, his voice filled with a mix of intrigue and warning. "You keep seeking the truth in the underbellies of Sunter. But these things are within you and not where you think they are. Uncover the hidden connections. Templar Solace holds the key to unlocking the secrets that lurk in the shadows."

A sudden noise startled them—the sound of approaching footsteps. Morgan and Shepherd spun around, their hands reaching for their weapons, but instead, they found themselves facing a darkened alley. The stranger had vanished, leaving only echoes of his presence behind.

Shepherd's voice was filled with disbelief. "Where did he go?"

Morgan shook her head, her eyes scanning their surroundings. "I don't know, but we can't dwell on it now. We have a lead, and we need to follow it."

With renewed determination, they gathered the newspapers and the flash drive, tucking them safely away. The alley seemed to close in around them as they hurried back to their car, the weight of the case heavy upon their shoulders.

The awfully helpful stranger had set them on a perilous path, and they knew the answers they sought could change everything.

\*\*\*

The scent of rain hung in the air as they arrived at their destination—the hidden heart of the Sumter's underworld. The dimly lit streets were lined with dilapidated buildings, their broken windows reflecting the decay that festered within.

They stepped out of the car, their senses heightened, and the tension palpable. Their footsteps echoed through the desolate alleyways, the sound swallowed by the thick silence. Shadows danced on the walls, hinting at the secrets hidden within the darkness.

Morgan's hand brushed against the cold brick of a building as they made their way deeper into the labyrinthine maze. Shepherd's fingers twitched with anticipation, a tingling sensation crawling up his spine. They were closer than ever to uncovering the truth, but the danger loomed ever larger.

Suddenly, a figure emerged from the shadows—an imposing silhouette bathed in darkness. A voice, laced with menace, echoed through the narrow passage. "So, you've come seeking answers, have you?"

Morgan and Shepherd tensed, their gazes fixed on the mysterious figure. This encounter held the key to unraveling the web of deception that had ensnared them. They exchanged a glance, their resolve unyielding.

"We want the truth," Morgan declared, his voice steady. "And we won't stop until we find it."

The figure took a step closer, their face still concealed by the cloak of darkness. A chilling smile crept across their lips.

"The truth comes at a price, Detectives. Are you prepared to pay ,"the figure's words hung in the air, the weight of their meaning settling upon Morgan and Shepherd. They shared a resolute look, unspoken determination passing between them.

"We've come too far to turn back now," Shepherd replied, his voice edged with determination. "What is it you want?."

A low chuckle echoed through the alley, sending a shiver down their spines. The figure stepped forward, the dim light revealing his features—sharp, piercing eyes and a face etched with the marks of a life lived on the edge.

"Very well," the figure said, his voice carrying a mix of satisfaction and menace. "But remember, the truth can be a double-edged sword. It has the power to set you free, or it can consume you entirely."

Morgan squared her shoulders, her eyes locked on the figure. "We're prepared for the consequences. Tell us what you know about Templar Solace."

The figure's lips curled into a wry smile. "Templar Solace... a name that carries both fear and fascination. They were a mere pawn in a game far greater than themselves. A chess piece manipulated by forces lurking in the shadows."

"Who is behind it all?" Shepherd demanded, his voice sharp with urgency. "Who orchestrated these murders?"

"A more powerful force!"

"Why?"

The figure smiled. "Only he can give believable answers to that."

"But…"

The figure paused, as if weighing their next words carefully. "To find the answers you seek, you must first navigate the treacherous underworld. There, you will encounter allies and enemies alike. But be warned, not everyone is who they seem. Trust will be tested, and loyalties will crumble."

Morgan's grip on her weapon tightened. "We're not afraid of what lies ahead. We'll follow this path, no matter how dangerous."

The figure nodded, a glimmer of respect in their eyes. "Then be prepared, Detectives. The road ahead is filled with deceit, betrayal, and a darkness that threatens to consume all who dare to challenge it. But within that darkness, you may find the truth you seek."

With those cryptic words, the figure melted back into the shadows, leaving Morgan and Shepherd standing alone in the alley. The sounds of the county seemed distant, muffled by the weight of their mission.

As they prepared to venture into the underworld, the pungent smell of decay mingled with the acrid stench of desperation. The touch of cold, damp walls sent a shiver through their bodies, while the flickering neon lights illuminated a path of uncertainty.

They exchanged a determined glance, their resolve unyielding. Together, they would face the perils that awaited them, no matter the cost. The investigation had taken an unexpected turn, plunging them deeper into a labyrinth of secrets and danger.

With each step forward, they knew the stakes had been raised. The game had become deadlier, the players more elusive—knowing that the truth they sought would test them to their very limits.

\*\*\*

The pitch dark street  stretched out before Detectives Morgan and Shepherd like a melody of secrets. Every step they took resonated with a sense of urgency, their senses alert to the dangers lurking in the shadows. The pungent aroma of desperation hung heavy in the air, mingling with the metallic tang of fear.

As they navigated the maze-like alleys, their footsteps echoed in the eerie silence. Graffiti-covered walls whispered secrets, while discarded needles and shattered glass bore witness to the darker side of humanity that thrived here.

Morgan's fingers brushed against the rough brickwork, the gritty texture a stark reminder of the harsh reality they faced. He glanced at Shepherd, his gaze focused and determined. They knew that trust would be a precious commodity in this treacherous realm, and they had only each other to rely on.

Their first contact awaited them at a hidden speakeasy, a place where whispers of information circulated like currency. The neon sign flickered above the unmarked entrance, casting an ethereal glow on the wary faces that came and went.

As they stepped inside, the heavy scent of whiskey mixed with tobacco enveloped them. The low hum of conversation filled the room, punctuated by the clinking of glasses and occasional bursts of laughter. The atmosphere crackled with an undercurrent of tension, as if everyone present was acutely aware of the delicate balance between survival and betrayal.

They scanned the room, their eyes landing on a figure sitting alone at the corner of the bar. Dressed in a worn suit, he exuded an air of weariness that seemed to seep into the cracks of his weathered face.

Approaching cautiously, Morgan and Shepherd took the seats opposite him. The man glanced up, his weary eyes meeting theirs. "Detectives," he said, his voice tinged with resignation. "I've been expecting you."

Morgan studied the man, noting the lines etched deeply into his face, the scars that told stories of past encounters with danger. "You have information for us," he stated, his tone a mixture of assertion and inquiry.

The man nodded slowly. "Information comes at a price, Detectives. But considering the stakes, I suppose we can make a deal."

Shepherd leaned forward, his voice low but commanding. "We're not here to bargain. We need answers."

A sly smile flickered across the man's face. "Very well, then. Templar Solace, the one you seek, was once a formidable player in the game—a mastermind orchestrating the moves from the shadows. But something went awry. Ambition overtook loyalty, and betrayal reared its ugly head."

Morgan's brow furrowed. "Betrayal? Are you saying someone turned against Templar Solace?"

The man's eyes darted around the room, his voice dropping to a hushed whisper. "Indeed. The power struggle among the criminal elite reached a boiling point. Someone sought to eliminate Templar, to seize their position and control. And it seems they were willing to spill blood to achieve their goals."

Shepherd's grip on the edge of the table tightened. "Who? Who is behind these murders? We need a name."

The man leaned back, his eyes clouded with a mix of fear and hesitation. "I can't give you that name just yet. The chessboard is still in motion, and you two are but pawns caught in the crossfire. However, I can offer you a breadcrumb—a lead that may guide you closer to the truth."

Morgan leaned in, her voice laced with urgency. "Tell us, then. What is this lead?"

The man's gaze shifted to a dimly lit backroom, tucked away in the depths of the speakeasy. "In that room," he whispered, "you'll find a man who holds a piece of the puzzle. A man who has information that can shed light on the shadows that loom over Templar Solace."

"Why should I believe you?" Detective Shepherd asked, studying the man's hardened face.

"Same way you believed him without asking any questions," the man responded.

"Who?" Detective Morgan chipped in.

"The one who sent you here. Weren't you?"

Detective Morgan grabbed Detective Shepherd aside, they talked in whispers and then turned to the direction the man showed them.

"I'll put a bullet in your pant if you fuck with me," Detective Shepherd brawled, pointing his gun to the man who seemed indifferent even with the threat.

Detective Shepherd exchanged a glance with Morgan, a shared understanding passing between them. Without a word, they rose from their seats and made their way towards the backroom. The air grew heavier with anticipation as they pushed open the door, revealing a dimly lit chamber filled with smoke and the murmurs of clandestine conversations.

Their eyes scanned the room until they found the man they sought—a figure shrouded in darkness, hunched over a table, engrossed in a game of cards. The smell of tobacco and stale whiskey hung in the air, mingling with the tension that radiated from the players.

Approaching cautiously, Morgan and Shepherd took their places opposite the mysterious figure. The room fell silent as the players regarded them with suspicion. The man's eyes flickered, a mixture of curiosity and wariness in their depths.

"We've been told you hold information," Morgan began, her voice steady yet edged with authority.

The man glanced up, his weathered face etched with the marks of a life entangled in the underworld. "And what if I do?" he replied, his voice tinged with a hint of defiance.

Shepherd leaned in, his eyes locked on the man. "We're on a path to uncover the truth, no matter the cost. If you have information that can aid us, it's in your best interest to cooperate."

A moment of silence passed, heavy with unspoken tension. The players around the table shifted uncomfortably, sensing the weight of the moment.

"I've never loved cops. But, I do admire your courage. Brazen. Seamless," the man said amid chuckles.

Finally, the man let out a weary sigh, his gaze meeting theirs with a measure of resignation. "Very well, Detectives. But remember, there are eyes and ears everywhere. I can only reveal so much."

He leaned closer, his voice a mere whisper. "The one who orchestrated these murders, the puppet master pulling the strings, is someone known only as the Shadow Broker. A name whispered in hushed tones, feared by those who know the depths of their power. They have a web of influence that spans far and wide, and they stop at nothing to protect their secrets."

Morgan's heart raced at the revelation. The Shadow Broker—a name that struck fear into the hearts of even the most hardened criminals. "How do we find them? How do we bring them to justice?"

The man leaned back, a wistful smile playing on his lips. "Did you say them?"

Detective Shepherd traded glances with Detective Morgan. "How do we find him?"

"To find the Shadow Broker, you must tread where few dare to venture. Seek the hidden enclaves, the forgotten corners of Sumter. Sadly, he might be closer to you than you think. No one really knows."

"Even Templar Solace?"

The man's eyes dilated in awe at the mention of Templar Solace. He seemed like one who just stepped on molten magma.

"No one," he responded, avoiding their eyes.

Shepherd's voice was resolute. "We won't stop until we find him."

As they rose from the table, the man's eyes followed them, a glimmer of hope mingled with a haunting resignation. "Be careful, Detectives. The path you tread is dangerous. Trust no one, for betrayal lurks in the shadows. The truth you seek may come at a higher price than you can imagine."

Morgan and Shepherd nodded in silent acknowledgment. They understood the risks, the treacherous game they were about to play. But their resolve remained unyielding. The hunt for the Shadow Broker had become personal, a quest that would test their limits and challenge the very foundations of justice.

Leaving the backroom, they returned to the crowded speakeasy, the weight of the task ahead settling upon their shoulders. The scent of smoke, the clinking of glasses and the low hum of conversation filled the air once more as Morgan and Shepherd navigated their way through the sea of faces. The sense of urgency pulsed within them, driving them forward into the unknown.

Outside the speakeasy, Sumter county awaited them with its dark secrets and hidden dangers. The night had grown deeper, the shadows lengthening as they stepped onto the rain-soaked streets. The scent of damp concrete mingled with the distant aroma of street food, creating an atmosphere both familiar and foreboding.

Their footsteps echoed in the deserted alleyways as they moved outside the alley. The flickering neon lights cast an eerie glow, casting elongated shadows that danced along the crumbling facades of forgotten buildings.

Suddenly, a figure emerged from the darkness—a silhouette wrapped in a heavy coat, face obscured by the brim of a fedora. The stranger's voice carried on the cold wind, its edge laced with a chilling warning. "Detectives Morgan and Shepherd, your journey ends here."

Morgan's hand instinctively reached for her gun, but Shepherd's firm grip on her arm halted the impulse. They exchanged a knowing glance, a silent communication that spoke volumes. They had entered a realm where trust was scarce and danger lurked around every corner.

"We're not here to play games," Shepherd declared, his voice steady. "We seek the truth and those responsible for the murders."

The stranger chuckled, a sound that echoed with a sinister undertone. "Ah, the truth—a fragile thread, easily manipulated, easily broken. But tell me, Detectives, can you handle the weight of what you will uncover? Can you face the darkness that resides within your own ranks?"

Morgan's eyes narrowed, determination etched on her face. "We will do whatever it takes to bring justice to those who deserve it and those who don't. Even within us."

The stranger took a step closer, his presence radiating malevolence. "Then prepare yourselves, for the road ahead is treacherous. The lines between ally and enemy will blur, and the price of your pursuit may cost you dearly."

Without another word, the stranger vanished into the night, leaving Morgan and Shepherd standing in the wake of his ominous message. The weight of their mission intensified, the gravity of their quest pushing them further into the depths of the city's underbelly.

As they pressed on, the scent of decay grew stronger, mingling with the acrid stench of desperation.

Their journey had just begun, and they were about to face a revelation that would shake the very foundations of their beliefs. The stakes were higher than ever, and the realization that the enemy may be closer than they thought sent a shiver down their spines.

# CHAPTER 20

## Mayan

D ETECTIVE MARY COPPER rowed her boat effortlessly. In her lit up office, her eyes fixed on the crime board covered with photographs, newspaper clippings, and notes. The room was heavy with the scent of stale coffee and the lingering echoes of unanswered questions. She leaned back in her worn-out leather chair, a habit she had picked up during her years as a journalist, and allowed her critical eyes to scan the evidence once again.

The unknown person had managed to connect all the murder victims to a chilling crime that had occurred on Friday, May 7th, 2009. A familicide, she thought. The word rolled off her tongue like poison. The crime had taken place around 8 pm, just like the recent string of murders. There was a reason behind the carefully chosen time.

Detective Shepherd and Morgan were so busy chasing leads that they paid no attention to the answers stuck within the newspapers they received even when the parts they needed to focus on were all circled with a red old highlighter.

Mary's fingers traced the contours of a faded photograph of the victims, a couple whose lives had been cruelly snuffed out. The brittle paper crinkled beneath her touch. Their faces stared back at her, frozen in eternal anguish. The details of their deaths sent shivers down her spine. Their hearts ripped open after death, the method mirroring the present murders. The missing hearts were no longer a puzzle; they were the mark of a twisted signature.

As she delved deeper into the case, Mary found herself drawn to the story of the familicide. The victims were not just random casualties; they must have been related to the  murderer's. She couldn't say for sure, but she knew she'd get her hands on more clues if she kept digging.

Her heart sank as she realized the magnitude of the revenge that was being sought. Someone had harbored this fury for years, and now it was finding expression through blood-soaked vengeance.

Detective Morgan, a rugged man with a perpetual five o'clock shadow, entered the room with purpose. His eyes met Mary's, and he knew she had made a breakthrough. "What have you got, Copper?"

Mary cleared her throat, her voice laced with determination. "I've discovered something, Morgan. The voice of the cop in the recording we found belongs to none other than Detective Hine."

Morgan was taken aback. The first recording belonged to Detective Brown. He at some points fed the murderer with information. However, the second one which seemed connected to the murders in the newspapers belonged to Detective Hine. It further connected the dots as to why he got murdered—why it all started from him.

Morgan's eyes widened in disbelief. "Hine? That can't be right. He was the one who orchestrated this whole damn thing."

Mary nodded, her gaze unwavering. "He's the key, Morgan. The main cop who made the familicide possible. His murder opened the way to the serial."

Morgan's brow furrowed. "Why would someone kill him? And more importantly, why would he beg to be kept alive and refuse his share of the robbery proceeds?"

Mary leaned forward, her voice dropping to a whisper. "Because he wanted redemption, Morgan. He knew what he had done, and guilt gnawed at him. Maybe he thought that by refusing the money, he could wash away the blood on his hands."

Morgan's eyes darted across the room, as if searching for answers in the shadows. "So, the murderer is seeking justice, not just revenge. But where does that leave us? How do we catch this person?"

Mary sighed, her mind racing with possibilities. "We need to dig deeper into Hine's past, find out what drove him to commit such an atrocity. There's an establishment, a connection that we've yet to uncover. That's where the answers lie."

The air in the room grew heavy with tension as the two detectives contemplated the magnitude of their task. The room was filled with the scent of anticipation and the weight of the unsolved.

Just as they were about to formulate a plan, a loud crash reverberated from outside the office. Startled, Mary and Morgan exchanged a glance, their senses heightened. They knew that sound was no accident.

They rushed out of the office and down the hallway, their footsteps echoing in their ears as they sprinted towards the source of the disturbance. Their eyes scanned the chaotic scene before them—a shattered glass door leading to the evidence room, papers strewn across the floor, and a faint trail of blood leading into the darkness.

Without a word, Mary and Morgan followed the bloodied path, their hearts pounding with adrenaline. The stench of fear lingered in the air, intermingling with the metallic tang of blood. The flickering lights cast eerie shadows on the walls, heightening the sense of foreboding.

As they cautiously navigated the labyrinthine corridors of the station, their palms grew clammy with anticipation. Every creak and whisper seemed amplified, amplifying their tension. The trail of blood led them deeper into the heart of the building, a chilling echo of the past intertwining with the present.

Finally, they reached a door marked "Restricted Access." It stood slightly ajar, as if inviting them further into the abyss. Mary exchanged a glance with Morgan, her expression one of determination mixed with caution. They knew that stepping through that threshold could be their last act.

With a deep breath, they entered the room, their eyes darting across the shadowy corners. The flickering fluorescent lights cast an ethereal glow on the scene that unfolded before them. On a cold metal table, Detective Brown's lifeless body lay, his eyes vacant, his soul silenced forever.

Beside the table stood a figure, shrouded in darkness, the scent of vengeance emanating from their every pore. Mary's hand instinctively went to her holster, her fingers gripping the handle of her gun tightly. Morgan matched her intensity, his muscles tense, ready to act.

"Who are you?" Mary's voice cut through the silence, her words sharp and commanding. "Why did you kill Detective Hine?" she asked. "And now him," she nodded to the lifeless Detective Brown. "What is this all about?"

The figure turned slowly, revealing his face—a mask of cold determination etched upon it. A voice, laced with both pain and fury, resonated through the room. "You seek answers, Detective Copper. But do you have the courage to face the truth?"

Mary's heart raced, her senses on high alert. "Tell us! We deserve to know!"

A chilling laughter filled the room, reverberating off the walls, as if mocking their desperate quest for answers. "You're right, Detective Copper. The truth must be revealed. But first, you must pay for the sins of your colleagues. Blood must be shed."

Before Mary and Morgan could react, the figure lunged at them with startling speed, a glint of a blade flashing in the dim light. The scent of danger engulfed the room as the struggle ensued, the metallic tang of blood mingling with the acrid smell of fear.

In the midst of the chaos, Mary's mind raced, her instincts honed by years of solving crimes. She fought back with every ounce of strength, her senses heightened to their utmost limits. The room became a battleground, a symphony of grunts, gasps, and desperate pleas.

But as the struggle reached its crescendo, a sudden searing pain erupted in Mary's side. She felt a warm wetness spreading across her abdomen, her vision blurring. With a gasp, she staggered back, clutching her wound, the scent of her own blood overwhelming her senses.

Morgan's voice, laden with anguish, filled her ears. "No, Mary! Stay with me!"

She's been stabbed.

The figure scampered into the dark.

As darkness closed in around her, Mary's mind raced to uncover the final pieces of the puzzle. The truth, just within her grasp, slipped away, fading into the void. She fought against the encroaching oblivion, her last thought a promise—to bring justice to the fallen, no matter the cost.

# CHAPTER 21

## Overtuned

I N THE DIMLY LIT ALLEY, the atmosphere crackled with anticipation as Detective Shepherd and his specially assembled Flying Squad positioned themselves strategically, ready to pounce on their target. They had received a crucial tip from the mysterious informant, a man who had been aiding their investigation from the shadows. The time for apprehending Walter had arrived.

As the seconds ticked by, tension thickened the air, each member of the Flying Squad on high alert. The alley was veiled in darkness, illuminated only by the faint glow of flickering streetlights. Every sound, every rustle of leaves, seemed magnified, heightening the suspense that hung over the scene.

A vintage red car pulled into the alley, its engine purring softly as it came to a stop. The door swung open, and Walter emerged, his features masked by a mix of arrogance and desperation. He was a man accustomed to being in control, but tonight, fate had other plans.

That night, he was to become at least a billion dollars richer. It was the night of his signature underground auction;where he'd sell out his most valuable consignments—cocaine and stolen antiques.

Detective Shepherd's voice pierced the silence like a knife. "Walter! It's over. You're under arrest."

Walter's eyes widened, a flicker of panic crossing his face before he quickly regained his composure. He scanned the scene, his gaze darting from one officer to another, searching for a way to escape. But the Flying Squad had him surrounded, their determination unyielding.

"I don't know what you're talking about," Walter sneered, his voice laced with defiance. "You've got nothing on me."

Detective Shepherd stepped forward, his gaze unwavering. "We know about your involvement in the drug trade, Walter. We know about the antique auctions used to launder the money. The evidence is stacked against you, Shadow broker"

Walter's façade cracked, a hint of fear seeping through his defiant exterior. He knew that his carefully constructed empire was crumbling, his reign of power unraveling before his eyes. Yet, he refused to surrender without a fight.

In a desperate act of defiance, Walter lunged towards the nearest officer, his fists swinging wildly. But the Flying Squad was prepared, their training and expertise shining through as they swiftly subdued him, overpowering his resistance.

As the handcuffs clicked into place, reality set in for Walter. His reign had come to an end, and the walls that had shielded him from justice crumbled to dust. The weight of his crimes settled upon his shoulders, erasing the smugness from his face.

Detective Shepherd approached, his voice laced with a mix of triumph and solemnity. "Your empire is in ruins, Walter. Your time as a puppet master is over."

Walter's gaze bore into Shepherd's, a flicker of defiance lingering in his eyes. "You may have caught me, but others will rise in my place. The cycle never ends."

Shepherd's expression hardened, a glint of determination gleaming in his eyes. "We'll be ready for them, Walter. The cycle ends here."

With those words, Walter was escorted away, leaving behind a trail of shattered dreams and broken lives. The alley, once a backdrop for his illicit activities, now stood as a testament to justice prevailing over corruption.

Detective Shepherd took a moment to breathe, the weight of the investigation lifting ever so slightly from his shoulders. The relentless pursuit had finally yielded results, and Walter's arrest marked a significant milestone in their battle against organized crime.

That was too easy. How can the Shadow Broker be that easy to get?

Detective knew the answer when Detective Mary Copper jolted him from his sleep with ceaseless pats on his shoulder.

"It's about time!"

\*\*\*

The air inside the abandoned warehouse was heavy with anticipation, as though it held its breath, awaiting the arrival of chaos. A single dim light swung from the rafters, casting eerie shadows on the chipped concrete walls. The room was a battleground, caught between the illicit world of drug trafficking and the high-stakes domain of stolen antiquities.

Walter stood at the center of the warehouse, flanked by his trusted associates: Callahan, the towering enforcer with a scarred face, Marcus, the wiry and quick-witted getaway driver, and Evelyn, the seductive siren who could charm secrets from the lips of the most hardened criminals. The tension crackled in the air like electricity as they awaited the arrival of their mysterious buyer.

They secured Walter as she wambled to the front of the hall, heading right to the table ahead. The table held his most valuable assets. Atop the table were suitcases containing consignment.

He swung around, turning to the faces gawking at him from behind. Men in luxurious suits, women in sleek stilettos. They were all out to buy the drugs and bid the antiques.

As white rays flushed through the warehouse, Walter announced. "Ladies and gentlemen, you may want to put on your goggles at this point. It is time to test the quality and rarity of what I'll be offering you on a silver platter tonight."

The device seemed like a light-powered carbon tester. Walter nodded to Marcus and he unboxed one of the suitcases, revealing a green gem lost in a glass case. It was Walter's most-priced antique for the night.

"Straight from the discovered ruins of the ancient Egyptian treasury, I bring to you *Cleopatra's Tears,*" Walter announced.

There were ruffled murmurs within the small crowd.

"This masterpiece, steeped in ancient history and unparalleled beauty, is a true marvel that deserves a place in the hearts of gem lovers and collectors alike."

As Marcus nodded to Walter, he made forward and carefully placed the gemstone on the device, changing the white beams to a dark blue hue. It changed the entire ambiance warehouse, leaving it with the aura of a nightclub.

"Behold the beauty, ladies and gentlemen. This captivating hue, reminiscent of the depths of the Mediterranean Sea, is a testament to the gem's exceptional quality and rarity. Its color is deep and intense, captivating the gaze of all who behold it. The Cleopatra's Tear radiates a sense of mystery and allure, mirroring the legendary queen's captivating presence."

In earnest, the bidding began.

"I'll take it for 5 million," a female voice announced.

"I'll top 5 more million to that," another voice countered. A male this time.

"20."

"26."

Unbeknownst to Walter and his crew, a clandestine informant had whispered their every move to the authorities. The law had conspired with an unknown man, whose true intentions were masked by the shadows.

The arrival of the Flying Squad, a specialized unit trained to dismantle criminal empires, was imminent. They moved silently, their footsteps swallowed by the warehouse's concrete floor, their faces hidden behind dark masks.

As the door creaked open, a beam of blinding light pierced the darkness, revealing a phalanx of heavily armed officers. Walter's heart raced as he surveyed the scene before him, the hairs on the back of his neck standing on end. The Flying Squad had arrived, and they were determined to put an end to his reign.

"Surprise, surprise, Walter," a voice echoed through the vast expanse of the warehouse. Detective Morgan stepped forward, a smirk playing on his lips. "Did you really think you could operate under our noses forever?"

Walter's face hardened, and he instinctively reached for the hidden pistol tucked inside his waistband. But before he could react, gunfire erupted, shattering the silence like a thousand breaking glass shards. Bullets tore through the air, ricocheting off metal surfaces and sending sparks flying. The warehouse became a war zone, a ballet of death and survival.

The bidders took to their heels, running for their lives. Sadly, the cops awaited them outside the building. There was no way out. Some fell to the bullet and some scurried into safety—at least waiting to be arrested alive.

The acrid smell of gunpowder filled the air, mingling with the scent of fear. Each shot fired echoed in their ears, a deafening chorus that drowned out all other sounds. Splintered wood, shattered glass, and crumbling concrete added texture to the symphony of destruction.

Callahan, the first to react, bellowed in rage as he charged towards the onslaught. Bullets whizzed past him, ripping through the fabric of his coat, but he pressed on, his massive frame a shield against the barrage of lead. His meaty fists swung with lethal force, connecting with bone and flesh. The officers fell before him like dominoes, their bodies limp and broken.

Marcus, agile and nimble, darted between cover, firing shots with deadly precision. His fingers danced across the trigger, his eyes fixed on his targets. He moved like a predator, anticipating their moves before they even made them. His wiry frame twisted and turned, evading bullets that seemed to be chasing his every step. The smell of sweat mingled with the tang of blood as his victims fell, one by one.

Evelyn, usually the master of manipulation, found herself out of her element. Her delicate features were etched with determination as she weaved through the chaos. Her fingers curled around the cool metal of a fallen officer's gun, and she returned fire, her aim steady and true. But for every officer she downed, two more seemed to take their place. It was a losing battle, and she knew it.

Walter's mind whirled as he watched his trusted comrades fight. He had been betrayed, out of time and out of options. The scene unfolded before him like a macabre dance, the interplay of bullets and bodies forming a deadly choreography. But he refused to let despair consume him.

With determination etched on his face, Walter made a split-second decision. He knew he had to make a run for it, to escape the suffocating grip of the Flying Squad. In the chaos of the firefight, he spotted an opening—an old rusted door leading to a narrow alleyway. It was his only chance.

As he sprinted towards his escape route, bullets whizzed past him, grazing his arm and tearing through the fabric of his coat. Pain flared, but adrenaline fueled his desperate flight. The cold touch of fear gripped his heart, pushing him to his physical limits.

Walter's senses heightened in the face of danger. The stench of burning gunpowder mixed with the metallic tang of blood assaulted his nostrils. The sharp cracks of gunfire reverberated in his ears, drowning out the pounding of his own footsteps. Sweat trickled down his forehead, mingling with the dirt and grime on his face, leaving a salty trail.

He burst through the rusty door, stumbling into the dimly lit alleyway. It was a stark contrast to the chaotic frenzy behind him. The sound of sirens wailed in the distance, a haunting reminder that his escape was short-lived. His heart pounded in his chest, his breath ragged and shallow.

As he stumbled forward, his hand brushed against the rough brick wall, the texture cutting into his skin. Every step sent jolts of pain through his body, but he refused to stop. He had come too far to give up now.

A series of rapid footsteps reverberated behind him, closing in. The Flying Squad had given chase, relentless in their pursuit. Panic gripped Walter's chest like a vise, his mind racing for a way out. He glanced around, his eyes catching a faint glimmer of hope—a fire escape ladder leading up to the rooftop of a neighboring building.

Summoning his last reserves of strength, Walter lunged towards the fire escape, his fingers wrapping around the cold metal rungs. He climbed with desperate determination, his muscles protesting with each movement. The weight of his choices, the consequences of his actions, bore down on him heavily.

Reaching the rooftop, he gasped for air, his lungs burning. The county sprawled out before him, a vast expanse of possibilities and dangers. But he had to keep moving, had to find a way to disappear into the shadows once again.

Suddenly, a gunshot shattered the night, followed by a cry of pain. Walter turned, his heart sinking as he saw Callahan collapse to the ground, a crimson stain blossoming on his chest. The world seemed to slow as their eyes locked for a fleeting moment, a silent exchange of understanding and regret.

The shock of the loss threatened to paralyze Walter, but he knew he couldn't afford to mourn. He had to keep running, to fight for his own survival. The knowledge that his every move was being tracked by the relentless Flying Squad spurred him onward.

With a renewed sense of purpose, Walter dashed across the rooftop, his legs propelling him forward. The night air rushed past his face, his body propelled by a mix of adrenaline and desperation. The distant wail of sirens grew louder, closing in on his location.

And as he leaped across the gap between buildings, his fingers barely grazing the edge of the adjacent rooftop, a single thought echoed in his mind: escape or capture, life or death. The choice hung in the balance, a precarious tightrope he was determined to navigate.

But little did Walter know that his escape had not gone unnoticed. High above the rooftops, a figure clad in black watched with keen eyes.Detective Shepherd.

Perhaps, Walter didn't know that towered ahead of him was the man who had long dedicated  his life just to find him.

Furious and pained, Detective Shepherd watched, giving him a close marking on every step he made.

He had seen it all—the shootout, the fleeting glimpse of Walter's escape. He came with the flying squad. He started it. He swore to watch it screech to an end—even at the point of death.

With the precision of a predator, Shepherd leaped from the rooftop, his body plummeting through the air before he expertly landed on the ground, just a few meters away from the staggering Walter.

He knew he had to close in on Walter before he disappeared into the night. Again, Walter snuck back into where came out. Shepherd didn't shoot. He wanted him alive.

Meanwhile, Walter raced through the labyrinthine alleys, his legs burning with exhaustion. His heart thundered in his ears, drowning out the sound of his pursuers. But the relentless echo of footsteps grew closer, signaling that the Flying Squad was relentless in their pursuit.

Turning a corner, Walter stumbled upon a desolate room within the warehouse, its doors yawning open invitingly. Desperation fueled his decision as he darted inside, seeking refuge from the impending capture. The smell of dampness and neglect assailed his nostrils as he navigated the dimly lit interior.

Unknown to Walter, Shepherd had been hot on his trail, a hound chasing its prey. The echoes of his footsteps and the faint scent of his sweat led him straight to the tiny door. The shaky doorknob was enough to tell that someone just sneaked into it.

With his gun drawn and senses on high alert, he entered cautiously, prepared for the unexpected.

As Shepherd ventured deeper into the tiny room, the air grew thick with tension. Shadows danced on the dilapidated walls, lending an eerie quality to the scene. Every step she took seemed to amplify the creaks and groans of the decaying structure.

The room had an opening at its rear. To Walter, he had a breakthrough, but a kick volleyed him to the ground the moment he stepped out through the opening at the rear of the room. As the figure pelted him with more kicks, he sprawled to the ground in surrender, grunting unendingly.

As he tired and blurry eyes fought to see who's before him, his eyes met a woman. Fair. Thick. Brown-haired. Daring. A woman cop.

"It's over, Shadow Broker," Detective Mary Copper said, pointing her cocked Glock at the helpless Walter.

"Get down," Detective Shepherd screamed but it was already late. Even though Detective Shepherd's jump sent Detective Mary to the ground, the bullet had already made it to her upper arm. It wasn't from Walter. It was from one of his men who escaped the violence inside the hall.

But, it happened that what they heard were two simultaneous gunshots. As the man shot Mary, someone else shot him. His brain was split open.

"Come on," the figure came into sight. It was Chief Siren.

"Get her to the Medic," he nodded to Detective Shepherd who first made it to his feet.

Walter wasn't gone. Swiftly, he jerked his frame and made to shoot but it all looked like the Chief had an eye on him since.

"That's enough, you asshole," he shot him in the chest.

Mary and Shepherd exchanged quizzical glances as Walter fell to the ground in loud stud. The detectives are shocked to see the Chief murder a suspect they've chased for weeks without getting all they need.

Noticing their shock, Chief chuckled and then patted Detective Shepherd on the shoulder.

"The Shadow Broker doesn't go about without a bulletproof vest. He'll be fine."

Now, that was more relieving than death.

## CHAPTER 22

### Over a Cup of Coffee

D    ETECTIVE MORGAN SAT IN THE corner of the cozy café, his mind consumed with thoughts of Templar Solace. The voice that had guided him throughout the investigation had been absent, leaving him with an insatiable desire to know more. Just as he was beginning to lose hope, a sense of restlessness settled within him, compelling him to seek solace in a familiar haunt.

As he sipped his steaming cup of coffee, Detective Morgan's senses were heightened, attuned to every sound and movement around him. The aroma of freshly ground beans mingled with the gentle murmur of conversation, creating a comforting atmosphere. It was in this sanctuary that Detective Morgan felt a tap on his shoulder, breaking the spell that had enveloped him.

Turning around, he found himself face-to-face with a waitress, her warm smile etched upon her lips. "Excuse me,

Detective," she said politely. "There's someone who would like to speak with you."

Detective Morgan's brows furrowed in surprise. He followed the waitress's gaze, only to find himself locking eyes with Templar Solace, who had quietly slipped into the seat across from him. A mix of disbelief and anticipation washed over the detective.

"You've been searching for me, Detective Morgan," Solace said calmly, his voice carrying a hint of satisfaction.

Detective Morgan nodded, his voice laced with intrigue. "Solace," he said, mouth-agape. He felt restless and shocked. He hoped to see everyone else on the planet but not Solace.

Solace leaned back in his chair, his gaze fixed on the detective. "I wanted to test your determination, your commitment to justice. It seems you possess both in abundance."

Detective Morgan leaned forward, his curiosity piqued. "Tell me, Solace, why did you choose to help me? What's your connection to all of this?"

Solace's lips curled into a cryptic smile. "Some questions are better left unanswered, Detective. But I assure you, justice has been served."

Just as Detective Morgan was about to press further, the waitress returned, her presence demanding his attention. With a nod of acknowledgement, he turned towards her, leaving Solace momentarily unguarded. But when he shifted his gaze back to where Solace had been seated, he found an empty chair—Solace that had vanished into thin air.

Confusion and frustration washed over Detective Morgan as he noticed a folded piece of paper left behind on the table. He unfolded it carefully, revealing an address—a ridge located in a distant county. The realization struck him like a bolt of lightning. Solace had disappeared, leaving behind another tantalizing clue.

"Justice is served," the note read, its words etched in cryptic ink. "But...you can cross over for a hike over hot coffee, Detective."

Detective Morgan's heart raced with a mix of determination and curiosity. Solace's bold words beckoned him to follow the trail, to uncover the answers he had been desperately seeking. The scent of anticipation hung in the air, mingling with the comforting aroma of coffee that permeated the café.

With newfound resolve, Detective Morgan left the café, the bustling noise of the patrons fading into the background. He made his way to his car, the engine rumbling to life as he set off towards the distant county.

The truth is always edifying and if seeing Solace would put them before him, he was ready to hit the ridge.

Slumping into the seat of his GMC truck, he mumbled;

*Truly justice is served.*

## EPILOGUE

### Shadow Broker

T HE INTERROGATION ROOM WAS A STERILE space, the harsh fluorescent lights casting a cold glow on the worn-out table and chairs. Detective Shepherd sat at one end, his gaze fixed on the man who had once wielded power and manipulation like a deadly weapon. Walter, a shadow of his former self, sat across from him, his eyes filled with a mix of defiance and resignation.

Detective Morgan stood silently by the door, her piercing gaze locked on Walter. She had seen through his web of deception, piecing together the intricate puzzle that led to this moment. Detective Mary, a seasoned investigator with a reputation for extracting the truth, observed from the side, her notebook open and pen poised.

"So, Walter," Detective Shepherd began, his voice a low rumble, "care to tell us the truth? We know everything."

Walter's lips twitched, a hint of a smile playing at the corners of his mouth. He leaned back in his chair, a posture of false confidence. "You think you know everything, Detective? You have no idea what I'm capable of."

Detective Morgan stepped forward, her eyes narrowing with intensity. "We have evidence, Walter. The fingerprints, the forensic analysis—it all points to you. We know about the murders, about how you used Solace as a pawn in your twisted game."

Walter's façade wavered for a fleeting moment, a flicker of uncertainty in his eyes. He shook his head dismissively. "You're mistaken, Detective. Solace was the one who killed them. He's unstable, unpredictable."

Detective Shepherd leaned forward, his voice tinged with urgency. "Enough lies, Walter. We've spoken to Solace. He told us the truth, how you manipulated him, used him as a tool to cover your tracks. The fingerprints, the planted evidence—it all points to you."

Walter's face contorted with a mix of anger and desperation. "Solace doesn't know what he's saying. He's confused, lost."

Detective Mary spoke up, her voice calm yet resolute. "We've uncovered the truth, Walter. We know about the antiques, the stolen treasures that belonged to Solace's parents. Your parents. You killed them, didn't you? You betrayed your own family."

A glimmer of realization crossed Walter's face, his eyes darting between the detectives. He seemed to recognize the futility of his denials. "They were holding me back, keeping me from what was rightfully mine. I had to take matters into my own hands. I knew you dirty cops will never buy my bid! I did it myself."

Detective Shepherd leaned in, his voice low and filled with a mixture of disgust and determination. "You used Solace's grief, his vulnerability, to further your own twisted agenda. You manipulated him, led him down a path of bloodshed. Why, Walter? Why did you do it?"

Walter's voice wavered, a combination of defiance and guilt lacing his words. "Power, Detective. It was always about power. I wanted what was rightfully mine, and I wasn't going to let anyone stand in my way."

Detective Morgan stepped closer, her voice cutting through the room with icy resolve. "Your reign of manipulation ends here, Walter. The truth has been exposed, and you will pay for the lives you've destroyed."

Walter's eyes flickered with a hint of resignation, a glimpse of defeat. The weight of his actions pressed heavily upon him, his façade crumbling before the relentless pursuit of justice.

But as the detectives prepared to close the final chapter on Walter's reign of terror, a chilling smile crossed his lips. "You think it's over, Detective? You have no idea what I'm capable of. This is just the beginning."

Detective Shepherd's brow furrowed, his grip tightening on the edge of the table. "You're delusional, Walter. Your games are over. You won't escape justice."

Walter's laughter echoed in the sterile room, a haunting sound that seemed to crawl under their skin. "Justice, Detective? You think you can contain me? I've left a trail of destruction, and it won't end with me. There are others, like me, waiting in the shadows. They'll finish what I've started."

Detective Morgan exchanged a glance with her colleagues, a silent understanding passing between them. They had underestimated the depth of Walter's darkness, the tendrils of his influence reaching further than they had imagined.

As Walter's words hung in the air, a chilling breeze seemed to sweep through the room, carrying with it a foreboding presence. Detective Mary shivered involuntarily, a primal instinct warning her of the imminent danger.

Detective Shepherd leaned forward, his voice low and steady. "You can't hide forever, Walter. We'll find the others, dismantle your network, and bring them to justice. We won't let them continue your reign of terror."

Walter's eyes gleamed with a disturbing mix of defiance and madness. "Good luck, Detectives. You'll need it. The shadows are patient, and they'll strike when you least expect it."

With those ominous words hanging in the air, the detectives knew they were facing a foe far more formidable than they had anticipated. The darkness that Walter had unleashed would continue to threaten their city, and their fight for justice had only just begun.

As they escorted Walter out of the interrogation room, the weight of their task settled heavily upon their shoulders. Detective Morgan's gaze hardened, determination etched on her features. "We won't let fear paralyze us. We'll hunt them down, expose their crimes, and bring them to justice. No one is beyond our reach."

As they walked through the station's corridors, the scent of coffee mingled with the hum of conversations, but the weight of their task settled heavily upon them. The fight against the shadows had just begun, and they were determined to face it head-on.

Printed in Great Britain
by Amazon

22995612R00191